PLANET GRIEF

PLANET
GRIEF

Monique Polak

ORCA BOOK PUBLISHERS

Text copyright © 2018 Monique Polak

Library and Archives Canada Cataloguing in Publication

Polak, Monique, author
Planet grief / Monique Polak.

Issued in print and electronic formats.
ISBN 978-1-4598-1568-1 (softcover).—ISBN 978-1-4598-1569-8 (PDF).—
ISBN 978-1-4598-1570-4 (EPUB)

I. Title.
PS8631.043P53 2018   jc813'.6   C2017-907928-x
                        C2017-907929-8

First published in the United States, 2018
Library of Congress Control Number: 2018933704

Summary: In this novel for middle readers, a group of young teens
gather for a grief retreat, where they confront their feelings and
try to understand how grief affects everyone differently.

*Orca Book Publishers is dedicated to preserving the environment and
has printed this book on Forest Stewardship Council® certified paper.*

Orca Book Publishers gratefully acknowledges the support for its publishing
programs provided by the following agencies: the Government of Canada through the
Canada Book Fund and the Canada Council for the Arts, and the Province of British
Columbia through the BC Arts Council and the Book Publishing Tax Credit.

Edited by Sarah N. Harvey
Cover design by Teresa Bubela
Cover illustration by Byron Eggenschwiler
Author photo by John Fredericks

ORCA BOOK PUBLISHERS
orcabook.com

Printed and bound in Canada.

21 20 19 18 • 4 3 2 1

For Dawn Cruchet, gifted grief educator and counselor, amazing friend. With love and gratitude for who you are and all you do.

ONE

Abby

The whole point of not speaking to someone is so they know you're upset.

Only Dad doesn't even notice I'm giving him the silent treatment.

I haven't said a word to him since yesterday morning. That was when he told me I'd be spending the weekend at some grief retreat for sad-sack kids.

"What about soccer?" I'd asked Dad. "I can't miss practice. Not if I want to make the team."

"This is more important than soccer, Abby," Dad said. "Isn't that right, Jupiter?"

Jupiter is our cat. He isn't talking to Dad either.

I tried reminding Dad he'd already forced me to see the school guidance counselor and that two visits to Mrs. Goldfarb's office were torture enough. But Dad made it clear I didn't have a choice.

1

We are sitting diagonally across from each other at the kitchen table. If Mom were alive, she'd be across from me, next to Dad. I try not to look at her empty chair or at the spot on the table where her plate would be.

Dad pushes the cereal box toward me. I pour some cereal into my bowl and grab a spotty brown banana from a platter on the table. I peel the banana and slice it in, leaving the peel on the table. Mom would never have been able to leave it there. She'd have gotten up and put it right into the compost bucket.

With just me, Dad and Jupiter in the house, that peel will probably stay on the table till it petrifies. We don't bother composting anymore.

"Is that a good idea?" Dad says when we're about to leave the house. "Wearing your soccer cleats?"

When I don't answer, Dad shrugs.

So what if I wreck my cleats?

In social studies, we learned about conscientious objectors, people who refuse to serve in the military for moral or religious reasons. Wearing my cleats is my conscientious objection to being forced to go to some loser grief retreat.

When Dad and I are walking along Sherbrooke Street, I think about how if Mom were here, she'd be stopping to scratch dogs behind their ears or check out the window displays at the fancy shops.

Dad is oblivious to dogs and dresses. Come to think of it, Dad is oblivious to most things.

He never held Mom's hand when they were out in public, and he didn't like to cuddle when they watched TV. Dad was never much of a hugger either. When I was little, I always knew to sit on Mom's lap because Dad didn't like it. So now, when out of nowhere he grabs my elbow, I totally forget that I'm not talking to him.

"Why'd you do that?" I say, shaking my elbow loose.

"Uh, no reason." Dad throws his shoulders back the way other dads do when they're trying to act dad-like. It's not one of my dad's usual moves.

That's when I figure out what he's up to—there's something in the window of the Westmount Stationery Shop that he doesn't want me to see.

I tilt my head so I can look over his shoulder. Hanging across the window is a pale pink banner that says *Happy Mother's Day! Tell your mom how much you love her! Best selection of Mother's Day cards in Montreal!*

I can feel my lower lip start to quiver.

"Abby..." Dad doesn't finish his sentence. I know it's because he doesn't know what to say to me. Dad hasn't known what to say to me since March, when Mom died.

A woman is walking toward us. She doesn't look anything like my mom. She's wrinklier than a fruit roll-up. My mom lived to be forty-one, and everyone always said she looked way younger, even when she was sick. It's the woman's suitcase that gets me. A small rectangular suitcase on two wheels that she's pulling behind her. It's the same size, color and shape as the suitcase my mom lugged around day and night—the suitcase that contained the ventricular assist device, or VAD, a machine that circulated Mom's blood when her heart couldn't.

I stop and scrunch my eyes tight.

"Abby," Dad says. This time he finishes his sentence. "You okay?"

I don't answer. Not only because I'm not speaking to him, but also because I'm not okay and Dad knows it.

I wait to open my eyes until I can no longer hear the sound of plastic wheels clattering on the sidewalk.

Dad doesn't press for an answer. I slow my pace so I don't have to walk next to him, only when I do that, Dad slows down too. When I try speeding up, Dad picks up his pace.

"Grief retreat!" I mutter.

Dad takes that as an opening. "I'm hoping it'll do us some good. Dr. Burton recommended it for us."

Dr. Burton is the first doctor Mom saw when she had a flu that wouldn't go away. It turned out Mom had a viral heart infection called myocarditis. Dr. Burton referred her to a cardiologist, who recommended a low-salt diet and plenty of rest, but Mom's heart kept getting weaker. The VAD was supposed to tide her over till her name came up on the transplant list. Except Mom was dead before that happened.

"*Us*? Did I just hear you say *us*?"

"Correct. *Us*. As in you and me. I'm attending the grief workshop too. It's possible I forgot to mention that part."

I groan. Bad enough that I have to miss soccer practice and spend a perfectly good weekend at some grief retreat. But now I'm stuck with my doofus dad.

"There's a special workshop for parents, but don't worry—we'll be in another room."

"Phew."

Dad frowns when I say that. I think he's insulted. "It's you and me, Abby," he says, shaking his head. "We're all we've got left."

"Is that supposed to cheer me up?"

Dad sighs. "I wasn't trying to cheer you up, Abby. I just want to be realistic."

I told you he was a doofus.

TWO

Christopher

"You look sharp," my mom says as she removes the key from the ignition.

I straighten my shoulders. *You look sharp* is code for *You look like him.*

Everyone says I take after my father. He's—I should say he *was*—tall and thin. Hearing the word *was*—even in my head—makes the muscles in my chest tighten. Like mine, Dad's eyes were two different colors. One brown, the other hazel. It's a condition called congenital heterochromia, and less than 1 percent of the population has it. Sometimes, when I catch my reflection, I get the feeling Dad is looking back at me. And for a split second, it feels like he's still alive.

I didn't argue when Mom asked me to wear a white shirt and my gray school pants to the grief retreat. I don't argue much anymore. Mom has enough troubles of her own. Why give her grief?

Grief.

It's been nearly two years since Dad passed away, and words like that keep following me around like a pack of stray dogs. *I nearly died laughing. Sudden-death round. The bass player's killing it.*

I check to make sure no one else is around to overhear what I'm about to say. "Do they all know what happened to him?" I've wanted to ask Mom that since she told me we were going to a grief retreat. I'm relieved I finally got the question out.

Mom's hand trembles when she takes my arm. The trembling is a side effect of the tranquilizer she started taking after Dad died and she couldn't sleep. Even though she's on a slightly lower dose now, she still shakes. "Only Eugene knows how Daddy died," she says. "He's the grief counselor who runs the retreat. He wanted to meet with me in advance because of our...circumstances. You'll like him."

Up ahead, a kid who looks about my age pops out of a green van. The driver is parallel parking, and the boy gestures that there is lots of room.

The van backs up onto the sidewalk. "Careful, *Mami!*" the boy shouts, waving his arms over his head.

My mom lets go of my arm so we can walk single file. I know what she's thinking: she's already lost her husband and she doesn't want her only child getting run over.

"Don't worry," I tell her, even though I'm pretty sure that won't make her stop worrying.

The boy is still guiding the driver into the spot. "Sorry," he says, shrugging when he spots us.

When the woman doesn't get into the spot on her next try, I offer to help. "I'll watch the back of the van. You direct your mom."

When the woman finally manages to park, I decide not to mention that the van is a foot and a half from the curb.

The boy shakes my hand. "Hey, thanks for your help. I'm Gustavo. Are you going to the grief retreat?"

"Uh-huh," I say. "I'm Christopher. Christopher Wolf. This is my mom."

My mom's hand trembles when she shakes Gustavo's.

"It's your first time at the grief retreat, right?" Gustavo says to us.

"Right," I answer for both of us.

"It's year three for me. This year, I get to be Eugene's assistant." It's obvious Gustavo is stoked about his promotion.

Gustavo's mom slides open the side door of the van, and a small girl jumps out. She is wearing a brown dress with yellow pineapples on it, and she has the same sleek, dark hair as Gustavo.

"Do you think we'll get teddy bears?" I hear the girl ask her mother. "We got teddy bears last year."

"That's my sister, Camila," Gustavo tells us. "She's six."

"I don't know about teddy bears, *mi amor*. But I'm sure you'll get something nice," her mother answers. She has an accent—Spanish, I think. Then she notices us standing with Gustavo. Our moms introduce themselves.

Gustavo's mom, whose name is Raquel, is wearing a necklace with a giant silver cross hanging from it. Usually, the only people who wear crosses that big are nuns, but I doubt she's one. Not if she has two kids.

Camila tugs on her mother's sweater. "What about an art activity? Last year we made a memory box."

The #24 bus pulls up on the other side of Sherbrooke Street. A boy and a woman I assume is his mother step off. I notice that when she reaches for his hand he says something, and she lets go. They pause at the corner, and the woman points at Lawrence Academy, the private all-boys school where the grief retreat is held. They must be going to the grief retreat too.

This won't be my first time inside Lawrence Academy. I was here in January for a chess tournament.

We need to cross Sherbrooke Street. Using his hand for a visor, Gustavo checks, then double-checks for oncoming traffic. He gestures for us to follow him when it's safe to cross.

"There's always an art activity," I hear Gustavo tell his sister. "Art activities help with the grieving process."

When we get to the other side of Sherbrooke, Camila skips ahead to join the boy and his mother. When we catch up, Camila introduces us. "These are my new friends Antoine and his *maman*," she says. Antoine has longish hair that gets in the way of his eyes. He nods hello at Gustavo and me without saying anything. The moms shake hands.

"Antoine has a maman and a mom," Camila says. "I know because I asked if his papa died, and Antoine said he doesn't have a papa." Camila looks up at Antoine. "You're the first kid I ever met with a maman and a mom."

"Camila!" her mother says. "What did I tell you about asking personal questions?"

"Oops." Camila covers her mouth with her hand. "I forgot."

Antoine shrugs. "That's okay, Camila." Then he looks back at Gustavo and Camila's mom. "She's a good networker."

Camila nudges her mother. "Can I ask him how old he is? Or is that a personal question?"

Camila's mom tries not to smile. "You can ask him that because he is a young man. It's usually wiser not to ask an older person his or her age."

Camila pulls on Antoine's arm. "How old are you, young man?"

"Thirteen, almost fourteen," he tells her.

"How old are you?" she asks me.

"Fourteen."

Camila beams. "Gustavo's fourteen too. I'm only six. That's eight less than fourteen."

A girl and a man I assume is her father are walking up the flagstone path to the school. The girl has bushy brown hair, and she's wearing a white T-shirt and baggy maroon soccer shorts. There's a hacky sack sticking out of her back pocket. I am guessing from her scowl that she doesn't want to be here.

Camila walks up to the girl. "Did your mami die?" she asks her.

"Camila!" This time Raquel sounds like she might lose it. I try not to laugh. Raquel shakes her head and whispers to my mom and Antoine's maman, "Last year she asked one of the fathers if he was looking for a girlfriend."

Instead of being offended, the girl in the soccer shorts throws her head back and laughs. She has a loud laugh. Her dad turns to look at her in a way that makes me think he hasn't heard her laugh like that for a while.

"What's your name?" the girl asks Camila.

Camila covers her mouth again, suddenly shy. "Camila," she says from behind her hand.

Gustavo rushes over. He must want to intervene before Camila says something else embarrassing. "I'm Gustavo, Camila's big brother. This is Christopher and Antoine."

"Abby," the girl says, extending her hand.

Camila pushes on the heavy wooden door to the school. "Last year we each got a teddy bear," she says. "To make us feel better."

When Abby catches my eye, I know it's because we're thinking the same thing. No teddy bear in the world is going to make us feel better.

Abby's father, a lanky man who walks with a slight stoop, helps Camila with the door. There is a round table in the middle of the lobby. On it are dozens of clay flowerpots filled with red and yellow tulips. Looks to me like we're getting tulips, not teddy bears.

The main office is at the end of the lobby. I spot a defibrillator on the wall by the office door. When your dream is to be a paramedic, you pay attention to stuff like that.

Before Camila can complain about the tulips, she spots a guy with a bad comb-over, wearing a tracksuit. He has on one of those bracelets that count the number of steps you take. "Eugene!" Camila shouts, barreling into him. "It's me, Camila!"

That's Eugene? I'd have pegged him for a gym teacher, not a grief counselor. All that's missing is a whistle around his neck. As I come closer, I get a whiff of way-too-much spicy aftershave.

Eugene squats down so he is at eye level with Camila. "I could never forget you," he tells her.

"I turned six in February. Mami says I got much bigger. This is Abby and her dad. They're both very grumpy. That's Antoine and his maman. He has a mom, too, but she's at home. That other boy is Christopher—that lady is his mami. Christopher helped Mami park. Mami is bad at parking." Camila turns back to Abby, Antoine and me. "This is Eugene. He's our grief counselor. Doesn't he smell nice?"

Eugene shakes hands with us all. "Christopher," he says. From the way he looks me in the eye I know he must be thinking about how my dad died. I look away. Now he's talking to my mother. "Mrs. Wolf…good to see you again. Welcome to grief retreat. There's coffee over there for the adults." He points to a table in front of the main office.

The moms and Abby's dad make a beeline for the coffee. A small crowd of other parents already huddle around the percolator.

Eugene claps Gustavo on the shoulder. "I was wondering when my assistant was gonna show up!"

Gustavo practically glows when Eugene says that. I wonder what exactly an assistant grief counselor gets to do. Some of the tulips look like they need water. Maybe that's part of his job description.

"I know what you're thinking," Gustavo says to me, lowering his voice. "Eugene doesn't look like a grief counselor, does he?"

Eugene tosses Gustavo a clipboard with a pen attached and asks him to tick off names as other people drift in.

When I peek over Gustavo's shoulder I can tell from the tick marks that most of the kids and their parents have already arrived.

"What's your last name?" Gustavo asks Abby.

"Lefebvre. L-E-F—"

"Got it." Gustavo ticks off Abby's and her dad's names. I can just make out a note in pencil next to Abby's name: *M-HD-Mar'18*. It doesn't take James Bond to crack Eugene's code. I bet *M* stands for mother. And that Abby's mom died of heart disease less than two months ago. No wonder Abby is scowling. Two months after Dad died, I was a zombie.

Gustavo makes a tick next to Antoine's last name, which is De Blasio-Cohen. Because Gustavo is resting his palm on the clipboard, I can't read the note next to Antoine's name. Gustavo nods at Antoine but does not make eye contact. I decide that whatever's in the note must be bad.

"You said your last name is Wolf, right?" Gustavo says to me.

I grab the clipboard from him. "Why don't you let me do that?"

Before Gustavo can object, I tick off our names. I also scratch out the code next to mine: *F-S-Aug'16*. I don't mind Gustavo knowing that my dad died twenty-one months ago. I just don't want him figuring out what the *S* stands for.

A girl with spiky, bleached-blond hair sails in. She is wearing a black T-shirt, black jeans and black sandals. Even her blue eyes are rimmed in black eyeliner. She looks around the school lobby, flashes a smile and announces, "I'm here for the grief retreat."

I toss the clipboard back to Gustavo.

"Just a second! I need to tick you off my list," he calls out to the girl.

The girl scans the list the way I did before. "There I am," she says, pointing a long black fingernail to a name near the bottom. "Felicia Symatowksi. It's a mouthful, isn't it?"

"Are you here with somebo—" Gustavo studies the list, and now he suddenly stops himself. "I'm really sorry," he tells Felicia, dropping his voice. "Both your parents. That's got to be the worst."

Felicia drops her eyes to the floor. Maybe Gustavo shouldn't have mentioned the parents. But when Felicia looks back up and says, "Thanks," I decide maybe the assistant grief counselor knows what he's doing after all.

There are thirty kids in all at grief retreat. Each one is supposed to be accompanied by an adult. But if both of Felicia's parents are dead, who will her adult be? Maybe she won't have an adult with her this weekend.

We're divided into six groups based on our ages. The younger kids will be in classrooms on the ground floor, and the older ones will meet upstairs. Gustavo, Antoine and I are with the thirteen- and fourteen-year-olds. Eugene will be leading us in a classroom on the third floor. Abby and Felicia are in our group too. They have already gone upstairs.

I wait for the other guys. Camila is standing on her tiptoes—she wants a hug from her brother. For a second I wish I wasn't an only child. Then again, if my parents had had another kid, that kid might have had an even harder time dealing with what my dad did than I am.

Gustavo talks the whole way upstairs. "What do you think happened to the Symatowskis? If they died at the same time, it was probably an accident—a plane crash or maybe carbon monoxide poisoning. Carbon monoxide is odorless, colorless and has no taste."

I don't tell Gustavo that I probably know a lot more than he does about tragic accidents. "I made my mami buy a carbon monoxide detector for our house," Gustavo is saying. "Do you guys have one?"

Gustavo doesn't wait for an answer. "If something happened to my mami," he says, shaking his head, "Camila and I could end up like Felicia. Orphans."

THREE

Abby

I don't know about Eugene. Maybe it's the Fitbit or the god-awful aftershave. Shouldn't a grief counselor seem a little more…well…serious?

Gustavo, the kid who checked our names when we came in, is arranging chairs in a circle.

Let me guess what's next.

Circle time.

Eugene claps. "Welcome to grief retreat!" He makes it sound like we've won the lottery, when we all know it's the exact opposite. We've lost the lottery. Big-time.

When Eugene leans back in his chair, the front legs lift off the floor, and I spot the jumbo-size Kleenex box he has stashed under the chair. "Before we introduce ourselves," he says, clapping again, "I want to say a few words about grief retreat. This is my ninth year with the program. It's offered twice every year—before Christmas, then again in May.

"As I'm sure you've discovered, holidays are rough for kids who are grieving. For those whose parents have died, May and June are an especially big challenge. Mother's Day is coming up"—my throat hurts when I remember the pink banner in the window of the stationery store—"and Father's Day's around the corner. Other kids are planning breakfast in bed for their moms or buying gym socks for their dads." Eugene pauses. "Grieving kids just want for it to be July."

If I wasn't a conscientious objector, I might nod. I picture the calendar on the back of our kitchen door. I so wish I could tear off the two top pages and make it be July. Or, better still, next July. Mrs. Goldfarb said grief gets easier to bear with time. Dr. Burton should have prescribed a time machine, not some grief retreat!

The boy across from me—Christopher—nods and says, "I know what you mean." Why is Christopher wearing school clothes? Maybe his grief has prevented him from realizing that it's Saturday.

"What most people don't understand," Eugene drones on, "is that when you're a kid and you lose someone you love, you feel like you've been exiled to another planet."

This other kid named Antoine says, "Yeah," like he knows exactly what Eugene means. "Planet Grief."

When Eugene smiles you can see the silver fillings at the back of his mouth. "Planet Grief! Good one, Antoine. Back on Planet Earth, kids are stressing about their math marks—"

"Or if they're getting the latest Xbox for Christmas," Gustavo adds.

Antoine shoots Gustavo a look. "Xbox? The controls on PlayStation are way easier to use."

Eugene is okay with interruptions. "Xbox or PlayStation," he says, "you get the idea. All grieving kids can think about is the hole in their hearts."

Did he have to put it that way? Anytime someone mentions *hearts* I think of my mom. If her heart had been stronger, or if someone else had died and Mom had gotten a new heart, I'd be at soccer practice or making a Mother's Day card. I wouldn't be spending the day here with these losers.

Eugene rubs his hands together like he's got big news. "Okay then. Why don't we introduce ourselves?" He pauses to make eye contact with each of us. I bet he learned that trick in grief-counseling academy. "Let's go round the circle and tell each other our names, something interesting about ourselves, and what brings us to this weekend's grief retreat."

Christopher crosses his arms over his dress shirt. He doesn't seem too thrilled about circle time either.

Eugene clears his throat. "Why don't I start? Something interesting about me is that I love working out." Does he really think we didn't figure that one out already? "I haven't missed a morning at the gym in ten years." He pauses. "I was exactly your age when my mother died."

That's when I take another look at him. Past the tracksuit and the Fitbit. I should've figured Eugene would have his own story of childhood grief. Why else would someone go into the grief-counseling biz? Not for the laughs, that's for sure.

"I had siblings who were a lot older than me," Eugene continues, "and I had my dad. They all wanted to protect me during her illness. It was cancer. In those days—we're talking over forty years ago—they didn't believe in giving kids information about illness and death. So it felt like my mom was there one day and gone the next." Eugene waves one hand in the air as if that's where his mother went.

"Afterward, there was no one for me to talk to. It took a lot of years—and a lot of hardship—before I did the grieving I had to do." When Eugene's Adam's apple jiggles, I worry he's about to cry. Luckily, he's got Kleenex handy. But instead of crying, Eugene looks up and asks, "Who's next?"

Gustavo raises his hand. No surprise there. "I'm Gustavo Lorenzo." He forgets that his hand is still floating in the air. "Something interesting about me is that I speak Spanish. My parents were born in Chile. This is my third year at grief retreat." He catches my eye and lowers his hand. "At first I didn't want to come. But my mami made me. And now, believe it or not, I actually look forward to it."

His face gets serious. "Most kids—and a lot of grown-ups too—don't know what to say to you after someone you love dies. Some people just stay away from you. That happened with this lady on our street. She's always outside sweeping the sidewalk in front of her house. She used to wave when I passed her, but after Papi died, she'd pretend not to see me.

That made me feel even lonelier. What I'm trying to say is…I don't feel lonely at grief retreat."

Gustavo runs his palms along his thighs. "My papi had lung cancer. He never even tried a cigarette. Not one. I still miss him every day. My sister, Camila, was only three when he died. Sometimes I think it's worse for her, because she doesn't really remember him."

I take out my hacky sack and juggle it with my feet. Eugene shoots me a look, but he doesn't ask me to put the hacky sack away. If he did, I'd tell him my soccer coach says juggling a hacky sack is good practice.

The girl next to me—her name is Felicia (we introduced ourselves when we were coming upstairs)—is playing with her cell phone. I think playing with a cell phone during a grief retreat is worse than juggling a hacky sack. Felicia lays her cell phone face down in her lap and starts introducing herself.

"I'm Felicia Sym…Symatowksi." She bites her lip. "Sometimes even *I* have trouble saying it." She snickers, then looks up at us. "My dream is to be a world-famous documentary filmmaker." She drops her eyes to the floor. "I came to grief retreat because my parents are dead," she whispers.

I start juggling double time. *Both* her parents?

"They died in…a snowmobile accident. They thought the lake was frozen over, only it wasn't. I was watching from the window of our chalet."

I let the hacky sack fall to the floor. Imagine watching both your parents die and not being able to do anything to stop it! How does a kid get over that?

"Who takes care of you now?" Gustavo asks.

Felicia pauses. It can't be easy for her to talk about all this. "My grandparents. They're cool—for old people. They're my mom's parents. They were broken up too, after the accident. But they say having me around helps." Felicia forces a smile.

Felicia is super brave. My dad may be a doofus, but being an orphan would be worse.

Antoine takes a deep breath. "My name's Antoine. I love video games. My favorite is 2K17. I'm here because my baby brother, Vincent, died a year and a half ago." Antoine speaks so softly that we have to lean in to hear. He pushes the hair away from his eyes. "He was only three months old. He was just starting to smile."

I realize I am pressing my fingertips into the bottom of my chair.

I can't stand listening to all these sad stories. What made Dr. Burton think grief retreat would be good for me?

"It was SIDS," Antoine continues. "Sudden infant death syndrome. Some people call it crib death."

Eugene looks at me and Christopher. We're the only two who haven't spoken yet. Christopher's arms are still crossed over his chest. Eugene must figure I'm the better bet because he says, "Abby, how 'bout you tell us something about yourself and what brings you here today…"

"You mean *who* brought me here."

Eugene runs his fingertips over his abs. I bet he does two hundred crunches every morning. "I guess you're telling us your dad made you come to grief retreat," he says.

"Correctamundo. I'm missing soccer practice." Then, because I figure I might as well get it over with, I tell the others what happened to my mom. "My mom died on March 15. She was waiting for a heart transplant. Which is weird, because you're basically waiting for someone else to die—in an accident or because of some kind of disease that doesn't affect the heart, like cancer." I look at Felicia. "Did your parents sign their donor cards?"

"Uh," Felicia says, "yes, of course they signed their donor cards. For sure."

When I finish, everyone turns to Christopher.

"My name's Christopher," he says. Only he doesn't say anything else. Which is super awkward.

Eugene is rocking on the back legs of his chair again. "So, Christopher, is there anything you'd feel comfortable telling us…about yourself and your circumstances?"

Christopher swallows before he speaks. "I play competitive chess. And my dad's been gone almost two years." When he crosses his arms over his chest again, I figure that's all he's going to tell us.

Gustavo shoots his hand back up in the air. "*Been gone* is a euphemism." It's clear he's proud to know the word. "A lot of people use euphemisms for subjects that are hard to talk about—like death. Right, Eugene?"

"It's true that *been gone* is a euphemism," Eugene says. Then he gives Christopher an encouraging smile. "But you guys can use any words you like this weekend. When it comes to grief, there are no rules."

"You know what kind of language I really hate?" Christopher says.

I think we're all surprised to hear him speak voluntarily.

"All the stupid crap people tell you after someone dies. At the funeral, this old man grabbed me by the arm and said, *Your dad is in a better place.* If he hadn't been so old, I'd have socked him in the mouth. My dad's not in a better place. The better place is right here—with me and my mom." Christopher's Adam's apple jiggles the way Eugene's did before.

Antoine nods. "When I went back to school after Vincent died," he says, "a teacher stopped me in the hall and said, *Your mom can always have another baby.* As if another baby could make us forget Vincent."

That reminds me of something a teacher told me: *Time heals.* She even pointed to her watch, as if an alarm would go off when my grieving was over. But I don't feel like sharing that with the others. Besides, they've got enough examples without mine.

Felicia wags her index finger in the air. "I have one too! After the…uh…accident, my great-aunt said, *It was your parents' time!* My parents were still in their forties. How could it have been their time?"

"You know what someone said that really bugged me?" Gustavo adds. "*You'll get over it.* Like I had a cold."

I groan. "I'd have said, *Maybe one day you'll get over being a total friggin' idiot.*"

I don't think it's just my crack that makes the others laugh. It's also the way I said it. Like I meant it.

I laugh too. In fact, I laugh so hard, I end up crying.

Gustavo reaches under Eugene's chair for the Kleenex box and hands it to me.

FOUR

Christopher

There's a ten-minute break after circle time. Because I really need to take a leak, I head for the boys' bathroom. The second I walk in, I spot a pair of black sandals at the bottom of one of the stalls. What's Felicia doing in here? Then it dawns on me. Lawrence Academy is an all-boys school. There probably isn't a girls' bathroom, though the women teachers must have their own bathroom somewhere in the building.

I'm about to leave (I don't want to embarrass Felicia) when I hear staticky sounds, followed by other people's voices. Who else is in here? And then, to my surprise, I hear my *own* voice saying, "My dad's been gone since last August," and then Gustavo saying, "*Been gone* is a euphemism."

I rap on the stall door. "Felicia! Did you actually record circle time on your cell phone? Because that is so wrong."

Felicia flushes the toilet before she comes out of the stall. "Hey," she says without looking at me, "I'm really sorry about that. I didn't realize the video setting on my cell was on. Don't worry—I'll delete it. I promise." She slides her cell into the back pocket of her jeans and slithers past me to the sink to wash her hands. Once that's done, she pulls out an eyeliner pencil from her front pocket and starts putting on more makeup.

"Video?" I say, and then I remember how Felicia was playing with her cell during circle time. "You were recording images too?" I am so ticked off, I almost forget how badly I need to pee.

"Oh yeah," she says, speaking to her reflection in the mirror. "But I swear it was an accident. I said I'd delete it."

"Delete it right now." I glare at her.

"Fine." Felicia takes her cell back out. She holds it in front of me as she hits the Delete button. "Happy now?"

The question catches me off guard. "Happy? Me? How could I be *happy*? At least you deleted the file. Now if you don't mind"—I point to the row of urinals—"I need to pee."

I consider telling Eugene that Felicia was recording circle time, but I don't want to be a rat. Besides, maybe it *was* an accident—and she did delete the file in front of me.

But when I walk back into the classroom, I decide I need to say something. The chairs have been arranged around a conference table, and everyone is sitting down. On the table is a stack of paper, a bunch of pens held together with an elastic, and a shoebox filled with felt pens.

I clear my throat. "Eugene. There's something I'm wondering about."

Eugene grins. He probably thinks I've finally decided to share the details of my dad's death. "We're all ears. Go ahead and tell us what's on your mind, Christopher."

"The things we talk about this weekend...they stay 100 percent confidential, right?" I make a point of looking only at Felicia's feet when I say this. She is tapping one sandal on the floor. In chess club, kids tap their feet like that when they can't figure out their next move.

"Absolutely," Eugene says. "You're ahead of me, Christopher, because confidentiality is next up on my list of discussion points. In fact, I meant to bring it up earlier. It's essential to our work together that this is a safe place." He uses his hands to draw an arc in the air. "Cone of silence. Whatever we talk about this weekend stays right here. Now, that doesn't mean you can't talk about your *own* experience. In fact, I'd encourage you to do that after grief retreat is over. But what you absolutely *cannot* do is share what any of the other participants bring to this grief retreat. Agreed?"

"Agreed," Antoine and Gustavo say at the same time.

Abby is juggling her hacky sack. "Agreed," she says as she catches it with her ankle.

"Yup," I say.

Felicia finally stops tapping her sandal. She looks up and gives me her best smile. "Agreed."

I wish I knew for sure that Felicia's cell was back in her pocket—not hidden under her T-shirt—and that it's not recording audio. If she wasn't sitting, I could check for a bulge in her pocket. I'll have to wait till she stands up to do that. Either way, my instincts tell me Felicia is hiding something.

Which means the two of us have something in common.

Eugene hands everyone a sheet of paper, and Gustavo comes around with pens.

"Not to worry," Eugene says, winking in a corny way. "This isn't a test, and there's no final exam tomorrow. We're gonna spend most of our time together this weekend doing creative exercises and sharing stories…"

Not if I can help it. Cone of silence or not, there's no way I'm telling a roomful of strangers about my dad's death.

No way.

"But I'd like to start by giving you guys some basic information," Eugene continues. "Take notes, if you feel like it. If you'd rather just listen, that's good too."

"What if we don't feel like taking notes—or listening?" Abby asks.

I like her spunk.

Eugene chuckles. "You've got a great sense of humor, Abby. And hey, if you don't feel like listening, go ahead and take a snooze. I'll wake you when we get to the good stuff."

Abby drops her chin to her chest and fake-snores.

"Grief's a roller coaster," Eugene says.

Abby shakes her head as if she's waking up from a long sleep. "There's no way I'm writing that down, Eugene. A roller coaster's fun. Everyone wants to ride a roller coaster."

Gustavo raises his hand. "Not someone with motion sickness. People with motion sickness hate roller coasters. I once saw a kid on the roller coaster at La Ronde puke his guts out." He pinches his nose.

"Those are excellent points," Eugene says. "What I mean is, we go through lots of ups and downs when we're grieving."

"Personally, I haven't noticed any ups," Abby calls out.

"Me neither," I say.

"Okay," Eugene says, "let me try this again. A person who's grieving experiences all kinds of feelings, sometimes even different feelings at the same time. After my mom died, I felt frozen. I also felt angry and sad."

Frozen. It's an interesting word, even if it reminds me of Popsicles. Maybe I feel frozen sometimes. And definitely sad. And sometimes also angry. But of all the words Eugene just mentioned, *frozen* is the one that sticks, maybe because it's the first time I've heard anyone use it to describe a feeling.

"How long does *frozen* last?" I ask.

"That's the thing," Eugene says. "There's no timeline. Grief is different for every single one of us. People used to think grief had distinct stages and that people graduated"— Eugene makes quotation marks in the air when he says the word *graduated*—"from one stage to the next. But now we know that grief changes all the time. Some people get stuck along the way. I was frozen for a long time."

I look up at Eugene. "How long?"

Eugene rubs his forehead. "About fifteen years."

"You're kidding," Antoine calls out. "That means I might not defrost till I'm twenty-eight."

So Antoine feels frozen too. Something about that makes me feel a little better.

"You'll defrost sooner if you tune into your feelings—and share them."

I'm relieved Eugene doesn't look at me when he says that.

"But a person needs to be *ready* to talk about his—or her—feelings." This time Eugene catches my eye.

I see that Gustavo has written the words *frozen*, *angry* and *sad* on his sheet. I don't know why he needs to take notes if it's his third year at grief retreat. Hasn't he learned all this already? Felicia is scribbling away too.

Antoine isn't taking notes, but he sure is nodding a lot.

Abby twirls her pen. She's made it clear to all of us that she doesn't want to be here.

I leave my pen where it is, placed to the right of my sheet like a discarded pawn by the side of the chessboard.

Eugene rubs his hands together. "Grieving," he says, "is a lifelong process. There's no getting over it. Ever." He shakes his head. "Even for adults, death is a lot to take in. It's even tougher for kids. I'll never forget how, in the first weeks after my mother died, I'd wake up and think every-thing was fine. The birds were chirping, the house smelled of coffee, the sun was streaming in through the blinds. Then it would hit me—Ma was dead. What I would have given to be able to stay in those first few sleepy moments."

Eugene sounds as if he wishes that, even all these years later, he could still return to those sleepy moments.

I know exactly what Eugene means.

I have had that feeling every single morning since Dad died.

That's when I pick up my pen and start taking notes.

FIVE

Abby

Ever met someone who talks in paragraphs?

Meet Eugene.

I bet when he's downing protein shakes with his gym buddies, he gives them advice about grieving too. Whether they want it or not. And I bet he asks them extremely personal questions. I pity Eugene's gym buddies.

"You guys talked about the stupid things people said after your loved one died. Is there more you want to say about feeling angry?" Eugene asks now.

Gustavo's hand shoots up like a NASA rocket. Someone should get that kid a T-shirt that says *Suck-Up* on it. "You know that neighbor I told you about? Sometimes I feel like ringing her bell and yelling at her."

Eugene nods sympathetically, as if he thinks that is a sensible plan. "I hear you," he says. "That woman let you down, although she probably didn't mean to."

"I also feel angry when I see people smoking." Once Gustavo starts talking, he can't shut it off. "They're alive and my papi—who never even tried a cigarette—is *dead*."

Christopher shakes his head. "It's just not fair," he says. "We were friends with this family—my mom and dad knew the parents from way back, and I was close with the kids. They're the ones who got me into chess. After my dad, uh, died"—I can see Christopher is trying to avoid euphemisms—"they invited us over for dinner once or twice, but then they stopped calling. When I tried phoning their house, the kids were always too busy even for a round of chess. This might sound crazy, but I felt like they were treating me as if I had some contagious disease. Like if we hung out, their dad might end up dying too."

Eugene nods. "Grief rewrites your address book."

"Address book?" Felicia is confused. "Oh, you mean your *contacts list*."

"Contacts list?" It's Eugene's turn to be confused.

"Your contacts list. On your phone." When Felicia takes her phone out of her pocket to demonstrate, Christopher glares at her. I don't know what he has against cell phones.

"In the old days," Eugene says, "when dinosaurs roamed the earth, we had address *books*. But I guess now I should say, 'Grief rewrites your contacts list.' Which reminds me—I was thinking we should make grief retreat a cell-phone-free zone."

Felicia groans. "That would suck. Do we have to?"

"Yup," Eugene tells her.

33

"I hate not having my phone," Felicia says. Then she adds, "For security reasons. In case my, uh, my grandparents need to reach me."

"You can leave the ringer on," Eugene says.

"I'm in favor of making grief retreat cell phone free," Christopher says.

We all hand our phones to Eugene, who piles them up on the middle of the table. I'm just glad he didn't make me turn in my hacky sack.

Eugene gets back to the point he was making. "Some of the people you were sure would be there for you *aren't*. That hurts."

"And some of the people you didn't expect to be there for you *are*," Antoine adds.

"Bingo," Eugene says. "Is there someone like that in your life?" he asks Antoine. "A person who surprised you in a good way?"

Antoine doesn't need to stop to consider his answer. "My *oncle* Etienne, Maman's brother. They were never close. Maman says it's because he didn't like her being gay. But after Vincent died, Oncle Etienne started coming by. He always brings soup. Carrot soup, broccoli soup, watermelon soup."

"Watermelon soup?" Gustavo asks. "I never heard of watermelon soup."

"It's really good," Antoine says, "once you get used to the idea that there's watermelon in it. Vincent died eighteen months ago, and Oncle Etienne still brings soup over.

So, yeah, he surprised me in a good way. It makes up for the jerks."

Antoine spits out the word *jerks*.

Eugene rubs his hands together again. "It's healthy to let your anger and frustration out. Those kinds of feelings only get bigger if we bottle them up. One year I brought a punching bag to grief retreat."

Gustavo raises his hand. "Wasn't that the year Tyler broke his finger?"

Eugene nods. "I told Tyler to wear wraps. He decided not to. You can put your hand down now, Gustavo."

Felicia is picking at her black nail polish. "I'm angry with my parents," she says softly.

I never thought it was possible to be angry with a dead person—or in Felicia's case, two dead people. I mean, it wasn't their fault. But Felicia thinks it was. "They shouldn't have taken the snowmobile out on the lake that day. They should have known it could be dangero…" Felicia can't get the word out.

I hand her the Kleenex box. When she starts sniffling, I reach out and squeeze her hand. She squeezes mine back.

"I'm really sorry for what happened," I tell her. "You lost—" Euphemism alert! "Both your parents died. That's got to be the worst thing ever."

Eugene jumps in. "Abby, it's great that you're able to empathize with Felicia." Is it my imagination or does he sound surprised that I am able to empathize with anybody? "But this is a good moment to point out something important.

Grief isn't a contest. We can't compare pain." Eugene pauses like he's about to say something deep. "Pain is pain."

Pain is pain? I almost laugh out loud. Even old Goldfarb came up with better lines than that!

Felicia dabs her cheeks with the Kleenex. "It's true," she says with a sniffle. "Pain is pain."

Eugene looks back at me. "How 'bout you, Abby? Do you ever find yourself feeling angry?"

"Nope," I answer. "Not really."

Gustavo rolls his eyes.

"Okay, Gustavo," I say. "The way you just rolled your eyes? That made me angry."

"Even your jokes come out angry," Gustavo says.

"I'm sarcastic. That's just my sense of humor."

I feel Eugene watching, deciding whether to say something or let us squabble, the way I sometimes let Jupiter squabble with the calico next door. If I don't step in, they usually sort things out themselves.

Antoine leans forward in his chair. "Were you always sarcastic?"

I don't answer because, to be honest, I'm not sure. Can a kid be born sarcastic, or did Mom's death make me that way?

"Sometimes my dad makes me angry. He's so…so…" I don't know why I just told them that.

"Annoying?" Felicia suggests. "My dad can—*could*, I should say, be really annoying. My mom too." She bites her lip and sighs. "Of course, I'd give anything to have them back.

Anything. I miss them so much." She wipes the corner of one eye.

"Yeah," I say, "annoying. And also out of it." I end up telling them more. "He never talks about how he feels. And he has zero sense of humor. My mom was the funny one."

Eugene gives another one of his sympathetic nods. "Maybe the adults' workshop will help your dad get more comfortable expressing his feelings."

"My dad wouldn't know a feeling from a French fry."

Gustavo is the only one who doesn't laugh. "See, that was an angry joke."

Eugene raises his palm in the air. It's time to separate the cats. "There's nothing wrong with feeling angry or frustrated or sad. But when we feel those ways, it can help to have an outlet. Joking can be an outlet. Sports or other kinds of physical activity work too. Abby mentioned she plays soccer, and I think I mentioned that I work out."

"I play video games," Antoine says. He pokes me with his elbow. "If you don't mind my asking, why are you wearing your soccer cleats to grief retreat?"

"Because I wanted to go to soccer today—not grief retreat."

If Eugene is insulted, he doesn't let on. He just picks up where he left off. "Playing video games can be an outlet too. Or chess," he says, and we know he's thinking about Christopher. "Art's another outlet. As a matter of fact, I think it might be time to do a little art."

Eugene wants us to draw a happy memory connected to the person we are grieving.

Which is when I discover something else that makes me angry. Felt pens.

I haven't used a felt pen since third grade. And I'm not about to use one now.

I'm hoping Christopher will boycott felt pens too. But when I look over at him, he is already busy making some lame drawing.

I point to a mysterious black shape on his page. "Is that supposed to be a chess piece?"

"It's a sewing machine. My dad was into fixing stuff."

"Sewing machine, huh? That was gonna be my second guess. So did he fix sewing machines? Or did he sew?"

"He sewed. He said it was relaxing."

Unlike Gustavo, Christopher is a man of few words.

"What kind of stuff did he sew?"

Christopher shrugs. "You know," he says. "Stuff."

"If I knew," I tell him, "I wouldn't be asking."

Christopher sighs. "He made our living room curtains. But he was mostly into fixing stuff. See this..." He pulls one leg out from under the table and shows me the knee on his gray pants. "He fixed a tear right here. I bet you can't even tell, can you?"

I have to look hard to see the tiny gray stitches. "Nice job."

Christopher cracks a smile. "Thanks." From the way he says it, you'd think he was the one who'd fixed the hole.

At first I think Antoine is drawing a fish tank, but then I realize it's an incubator with a baby inside. That must be Vincent. When Antoine adds two women and a boy, I realize he is making a family portrait.

Felicia checks out Antoine's drawing too. "Isn't it embarrassing," she asks him, "having two mothers?"

There's something mean about Felicia's tone—like she's laughing on the inside. But Antoine doesn't let it get to him. He doesn't bother looking up from his drawing. "I don't have a problem with it," he says.

Felicia has drawn a canopy bed with a little girl in it. Her parents are hovering on either side—kind of like angels, which I find creepy. But at least Felicia can draw. The girl really looks like her, right down to the black eyeliner.

Gustavo may be trying to draw a bicycle, though it's hard to know. When he catches me peering over his shoulder, he asks, "What are you going to draw, Abby?"

"Nothing," I tell him. "Felt pens are for babies."

Antoine turns to look at me. Oops. Why'd I have to say *babies*?

"I mean, I'm too old for felt pens."

Eugene taps my elbow. "You too old for charcoal?" Eugene hands me a cardboard packet with six charcoal pencils inside.

I run the edge of one of the pencils along my sheet. When my elbow accidentally grazes the line I've drawn, it smudges. There is something I like about the black blur I've made.

At first I can't think of a happy memory to draw. All I can remember is my mom being sick. Weak, usually in bed, the way she was at the end, struggling even to sit up. I have to search farther back to remember when she was healthy. The old mom. The one I thought I'd always have.

And then, out of nowhere, a good memory comes.

It's my birthday. Mom cuts me the first slice of the chocolate cake she made for me. I nearly gag when I taste it.

"Don't you like it, Abby?" she asks.

Mom takes her fork and helps herself to a corner of my slice. She spits it into her napkin. "Oh my god," she says, covering her mouth. "I forgot the sugar." Then she laughs so hard she has to hold her sides.

I turn the charcoal smudge into a flame and sketch a candle under it.

I can feel Eugene watching me. I move my sheet of paper away so he won't be able to see it.

I really hope he's not going to ask us to share our memories, but then he clears his throat. "Maybe you'd like to say something about your drawings."

I turn my drawing over. "I wouldn't."

Gustavo looks up at me and sighs. "You could try being a little nicer. You can trust Eugene—and the rest of us too."

"I don't know if we can trust *everybody* here," Christopher mutters.

Eugene raises his palm in the air. "I appreciate your running interference, Gustavo, but Abby, you don't need to worry about being nice. Just take your time. We've got all weekend. As for trust, that takes time too. And if any of you decide not to share what you're going through, that's okay. We're not here to push anybody into doing anything they don't want to." I'm pretty sure the *we* is meant for Gustavo.

Gustavo doesn't get the message. His hand is back in the air. "Even Eugene has trouble sharing some parts of his story," he says.

This time Eugene sighs. Something tells me he'd like to fire his assistant.

SIX

Christopher

I slide closer to the table and prop my chin on my hands. Maybe I'm not the only one at grief retreat who has trouble *sharing*. It's starting to look like Eugene has a secret of his own.

Antoine rests his chin on his hands too. Abby's eyes are glued to Eugene's face.

"So what's the part of your story that's so hard for you to tell?"

I swear, if Felicia was a dog she'd be drooling.

Eugene plays with his Fitbit. I bet he wishes he could be racking up another thousand steps right now instead of pouring out his guts to a bunch of kids.

Felicia has added pillows to the bed in her drawing. But now she puts down her pen and eyes her cell phone on the table. I bet she wishes she could record whatever Eugene is about to tell us.

Gustavo bites his lower lip. "Uh, I'm sorry, Eugene. Maybe I shouldn't have said anything."

Eugene pats Gustavo's shoulder. "Don't worry, bud. I might have waited a little longer to share that information. It's pretty personal. But hey, I might as well tell it now. Get it outta the way."

Eugene stretches his legs underneath the table, crossing them at the ankle. He takes a deep breath, then exhales slowly. "Okay then—here goes. It was 1972 when Ma died. Like I said before, I had nobody to talk to about how much I missed her. My father buried himself in his work." Eugene stops in midsentence. "That's the perfect word...*buried* himself...because after Ma died, he pretty much died too. My older sibs were busy with their own lives. Eloise had a new baby. Bill was engaged. None of my friends had a parent who'd died.

"Even our minister—our minister, for goodness' sake— he told me, *Eugene, you need to put this behind you.* He didn't understand you can't do that after a loved one dies. You can't just *put it behind you.*" Eugene raises his voice, but only for a second. "Basically, I grew up without ever having dealt with the loss. I went to high school. Did a year of college. But I didn't see much point in studying. To be honest, I didn't see much point in anything. I got myself a factory job. Eventually I got promoted to foreman. But something inside me didn't feel right—and I didn't know what that something was. I had no words for it."

"You were living on Planet Grief," Antoine says softly.

"I sure was. Only I didn't know it. Then in 1992, after my father died, I went into a tailspin. I think it was all the pent-up grief that never got expressed." Eugene pauses, and I know he is coming to the part of the story that is hardest to tell.

"I ended up homeless."

I sit up in my chair. Eugene homeless? No way. I can't picture it.

Antoine sucks in his breath. "You're kidding."

"I wish I was," Eugene says. "I lived on the streets for nearly four years. Those were the toughest four years of my life."

Felicia shivers. "Even in the winter? That's amazing."

I turn to look at Felicia. "*Amazing*? Did you just say *amazing*? Don't you have feelings?"

Felicia looks insulted. "Of course I have feelings."

Gustavo rolls his eyes. "If you two don't mind…Eugene was in the middle of his story."

"I lived on the streets even in the winter," Eugene continues. "Except for the really cold nights when I'd go to a shelter and spend a night or two inside."

Felicia pulls a black hoodie out of her backpack and throws it over her shoulders. "That would make a sick movie." When she catches me looking at her, she adds, "Or book."

"I don't know about that," Eugene says. "Most people make a lot of judgments about someone who lives on the streets—or even about someone who *used* to live on the streets. That's why I don't talk about it too much. No one likes to be judged."

That's when something makes me say, "My dad worked with homeless people." I already wish I could take back the words. I don't want to say too much about my dad.

"Oh yeah?" Eugene sounds impressed. I guess my mom didn't tell him that part. "Do you want to tell us about the kind of work your dad did?" When Eugene brushes his hand through the air, I notice how veiny his forearms are. "Only if you're comfortable saying…"

"He was a paramedic." This time I'm the one who needs to take a deep breath. I don't know why, but telling the others about my dad's job is taking something out of me.

"That's one of the professions I admire the most," Eugene says. "Paramedics do amazing work—and most people take them totally for granted."

"I'm going to be a paramedic one day too." My voice is so low it is almost a whisper.

"That's great," Eugene says.

I shouldn't have told the others my dad was a paramedic. Or that he liked fixing stuff.

Mom said Eugene knows how my dad died. But what if the others figure it out?

Paramedics fix things. They're often the first responders at accident or crime scenes. Things can get pretty gruesome. My dad prevented lots of people from bleeding to death, and he administered oxygen when they couldn't breathe. But when the trauma got to be too much and my dad was the one who needed fixing, he didn't know how to ask for help. That's the sort of person he was.

I would never have guessed that Eugene lived on the streets. He may wear too much aftershave, he may have the world's worst comb-over, but Eugene has been through a lot. Four years. Four Montreal winters. You have to respect that.

Dad cared a lot about homeless people. He said they weren't any different from us except they'd had worse luck. I remember him telling me how one homeless man he got called to treat had been a high-powered stockbroker. I remember, too, Dad telling me about a homeless woman who lived in a cardboard box, the kind a refrigerator comes in. The box stank so bad that Dad had to use his Vicks inhaler before he went in to collect the woman after she'd had a stroke.

Gustavo raises his hand. "Tell them how you turned your life around," he says to Eugene. "That's my favorite part."

I'm dying to—I mean, I'm really curious to know how Eugene got off the streets.

"Yeah, how *did* you turn your life around?" Antoine asks.

Eugene uncrosses his feet and leans back into his chair. This part must be easier to tell. "There was a rusty white van that used to come round at night. Back then, there were a few of us sleeping under an underpass by Highway 20. There was a nurse in the van, and an outreach worker. In winter they'd bring us coffee—and thick socks. Most people don't realize how quickly socks wear out when you live on the streets. It comes from all the walking. Anyway, I got friendly with the outreach worker. Her name was Myrna. In fact, we're still friends.

"Myrna was the first person I ever talked to about my ma's death and the hole it had left in my heart." I look over at Abby, but she's so focused on Eugene's story that she doesn't seem to have noticed he used the word *heart*. "Myrna was the one who told me about a support group for people with unresolved grief issues. There were about a dozen of us, and we met once a week for three months at the Y downtown. Everything started to change once I got that support. That was also when I started working out, and when I started to dream about going back to university and becoming a grief counselor. It took a long time, and I had to work really hard, but I got a lot of support—and eventually I found a way to make it happen."

"Are you still friends with any of those people from the support group?" I ask. I could see staying friends with Abby. Antoine's all right too. I'm so-so about Gustavo. I'd never want to stay friends with Felicia. What good is a friend you can't trust?

Eugene strokes his T-shirt over his six-pack. When he looks up at me, he's grinning. "You could say so. I met Denise in that support group. The two of us got married in 1999. She's the best thing that ever happened to me. Well, her and the twins. Michelle and Todd. They just turned fifteen. Luckily, they don't look anything like their old man."

"You look okay," Gustavo jumps in. "Though Mami says you shouldn't wear your hair like that."

Abby leans into the table. "I don't know about your hair, Eugene. But if I were you and I had twins, I'd worry they might inherit my exercise obsession. If you don't mind my asking—do Michelle and Todd wear Fitbits?"

Abby's deadpan delivery cracks me up. But I swallow my laughter when I hear the word in my head. *Dead*pan.

SEVEN

Abby

Ever notice how some people don't laugh at their own jokes? I laugh harder at my *own* jokes than anyone else's.

There's only one bad thing about laughing. It makes me miss Mom. She used to laugh so hard that saliva would dribble from her mouth and pool up on her chin. It sounds gross, but I always thought it was cute. When I teased her about it, she'd laugh even harder. Now whenever I see someone laugh, I check for a little pool of saliva. I haven't seen one yet.

Grief retreat isn't working for me. I'm never going to miss Mom any less. So far, the only good thing about being stuck here all weekend is making friends with Felicia. Also, what Eugene just told us about living on the streets was really interesting. Felicia's right—it would make a sick movie.

It's also cool that Christopher wants to be a paramedic like his dad. I bet Christopher's dad died on the job.

Maybe he was trying to save someone *else's* life. That would explain why Christopher is too upset to talk about what happened.

Somewhere in the distance, I hear the piercing sound of an ambulance siren. In a big city like Montreal, we hear ambulances all the time. But because of what Christopher just told us, I pay more attention. The sound gets louder, then even louder. Felicia rushes to the window and peers out. "I wish I could see what's going on," she says.

Christopher's shoulders tense up. He only relaxes after the ambulance passes the school and the sound of the siren fades.

Felicia shrugs and goes to sit back down. I think she's disappointed that the action's over.

"My mami freaks out when she's driving and she hears an ambulance," Gustavo says.

Gustavo can't handle silence. When the classroom gets quiet (like it did after Eugene's story), Gustavo jumps in to fill the empty space. My mom's aunt Gina is that way too. Mom and I used to make a game of it. When Gina came for dinner and there was a lull in the conversation, Mom and I would always look at each other. We knew Aunt Gina was about to start talking.

"My mami's not the best driver," Gustavo says. "If it weren't for Christopher, she'd still be outside trying to park."

Antoine clasps and unclasps his hands. Then he clears his throat. "The paramedics came to our house the night Vincent died. But there wasn't anything they could do to bring him back. My mothers screamed so loud it woke up our downstairs neighbors." The way Antoine is blinking makes me think he's trying not to cry. "That's what I remember every time I hear an ambulance."

"I'm so sorry," Eugene says quietly.

Felicia lays her palms on the table. "Just look at it this way—it would have been worse if Vincent was older," she says.

"Fel—" Eugene starts to say something, but Antoine interrupts him.

"Why?" Antoine asks Felicia. He may not have minded when she made that comment before about having two mothers, but now his eyes are flashing. "Why would it have been worse if Vincent was older?"

Felicia looks at Antoine. "Because you'd have loved him more."

Antoine's spine straightens. I know what Felicia means, but she shouldn't have said it. For a second I worry that Antoine is going to jump out of his seat, but then he settles down. "You don't get it, Felicia, do you? I'll never get to love Vincent more. That's the hardest part."

Eugene pats Antoine's back. "I think Felicia gets it now, Antoine. You've explained things very well. When someone young dies, or in Vincent's case, someone very, very young, we don't just mourn the person, we mourn the moments we'll never have together."

"I didn't mean to upset you," Felicia says.

It isn't exactly an apology.

Antoine nods.

That gets me thinking about all the moments I'll never have with Mom. She'll never come to another soccer practice, and she won't be at my high-school graduation or my wedding—if I ever decide to get married.

Christopher looks over at Eugene. "My dad taught other paramedics. I always dreamed I'd be in his class someday. So that's one of the moments I'll never have."

Christopher is coming out of his shell. Or maybe he just likes talking about paramedics. "You know what Gustavo said before about his mom wanting to get out of the way when she hears a siren? That's how most people react," he says. "They don't give much thought to where the ambulance is headed. Or to the paramedics on the bus."

"The bus?" I say.

"That's what paramedics call it."

"A day in the life of a paramedic would make an awesome movie," Felicia says.

"Is that all you think about?" The angry way Christopher asks the question tells me again that he doesn't like Felicia. I don't get why. She's not exactly tactful, but that isn't a reason to hate her.

I want Felicia to know I think she's okay, so I say, "I'd definitely go see a movie about a paramedic."

Eugene gives Felicia a long look. "Christopher's right though. You seem to see everything as if it's a scene in a movie."

"Uh, yeah." Felicia is staring at the floor again. She does that a lot. "I have this amazing media-studies teacher. We got to make a three-minute documentary. You'd be surprised how much work goes into a three-minute video."

"What was your documentary about?" Eugene asks.

"We interviewed my grandmother. When she was young, she was a reporter for the *Montreal Star*. She told us how she used to hunt for stories. We called our video *Story Hunter*. It's an interview with my grandmother, with still shots of old newspaper clippings."

"Is that the grandmother you live with?" The way Christopher asks the question reminds me of a lawyer on TV, interrogating a witness on the stand.

For a second, Felicia seems flustered. Maybe she got spooked by Christopher's lawyer voice. Or maybe she's remembering how she had to move in with her grandparents after her parents drowned. "Right," she finally says. "Same grandmother."

I expect Gustavo to say something, but now he is staring out the classroom window. When I turn to see what has caught his attention, I notice a boy on a bicycle. The boy's parents are walking behind him, holding hands.

Antoine notices Gustavo staring out the window too. "Hey," he says to Gustavo, "why'd you draw a bicycle?"

Gustavo comes back to the table and picks up his drawing. He holds it up for all of us to see. "That's my papi."

He points to a stick man wearing a pointy black hat. Hopefully, Gustavo's papi did not wear a witch's hat in real life.

"I was remembering the day I learned to ride a bike. My papi took off the training wheels, but he was worried I would fall, so he ran next to me. I still remember the exact second I learned to ride by myself."

"That's a lovely story," Eugene says.

Christopher makes a grumbling sound. "Maybe Felicia can make a film about it."

"What do you think your drawing means?" Eugene asks Gustavo. Eugene must see something in it or he wouldn't have asked.

Gustavo's eyebrows scrunch together when he's thinking. "I know I felt proud."

"Why were you proud?" Eugene asks.

It's not hard to see where this is going.

"Because I learned to ride by myself. Because I was independent."

"And your *poppy*..." Eugene's voice is gentle, but his Spanish accent sucks. "Was he happy about it too?"

"For sure he was happy," Gustavo says. "Papi wanted me to be independent. Ohh." Gustavo shakes his index finger in the air. "You think that's why I made the drawing? Because I want my papi to be proud of me?"

"I think if your papi knew how well you were doing and what a good brother you are to Camila, he'd be extremely proud of you," Eugene says.

Gustavo looks at the stick man with the witch's hat. "Thanks, Papi." Then he turns back to us. "My papi was born in Chile. That's where he met my mami. At university in Santiago, the capital city."

Christopher rolls his felt pen along the table. "Did anyone ever tell you that you talk a lot, Gustavo?"

Felicia gives Christopher the hairy eyeball. "Did anyone ever tell you that you talk too little? And when you do talk, you can be kinda mean?"

"Me? Mean?" Christopher shoots back. "At least I don't go around rubbernecking when an ambulance goes by. I don't get a thrill from other people's troubles."

"All right, folks," Eugene says, "let's play nice this weekend. Remember what I told you about this being a safe space? We create a safe space by being kind to one another— and not judging."

"And respecting confidentiality," Christopher adds. He gives Felicia a nasty look.

What's all that about?

"That's right," Eugene says. "Silence makes some people uncomfortable." We all know *some people* means Gustavo. "Sometimes, though, it's good to sit through the uncomfortable feelings. Gustavo,"—Eugene's voice is extra gentle— "some people don't like when it gets too quiet. Usually it's because the quiet reminds them of something else. Does quiet remind you of anything, Gustavo?"

When Gustavo answers, his voice sounds different, as if it is coming from far away. "Our house got really quiet after Papi was diagnosed. My mami stopped singing. A lot of people came to visit, but they didn't talk a lot. They just sat in the living room and held my parents' hands. For a while, Camila stopped talking altogether."

Thanks, Gustavo. You just set me up for my next joke. "I think it's safe to say Camila got over that problem. She made a full recovery."

Eugene chuckles, but his face turns serious when he looks at me. "You know how silence is a trigger for Gustavo—that it makes him uncomfortable? We've all got triggers, Abby. I'm wondering whether witnessing someone else's sadness might be yours."

EIGHT

Christopher

Someone knocks at the classroom door. The assistant grief counselor jumps up from his seat to answer.

"Hey, *hermanita*," Gustavo says. *Hermanita* must be Spanish for *little sister*. "I was just talking about you to the other kids. It's a sign that you came knocking."

Maybe it's a sign that it's snack time. I hear the ice rattling inside the pitcher of lemonade Camila is carrying on a round tray. "Don't spill," she warns her brother when he takes the tray from her, "or you'll make the floor sticky. Are the other kids nice? Mami says the girl in the black T-shirt is too young to dye her hair and wear so much eye makeup."

Felicia snorts. Then she turns to the window, studies her reflection and gives herself an approving smile.

"I like the blonde," I hear Abby tell Felicia. Why does Abby have to act like some groupie around Felicia?

"It's very"—Abby stops to find the word she's looking for—"dramatic. Your clothes too."

"Thanks," Felicia says. "Though I don't know if it's a compliment coming from *you*. Those soccer shorts and cleats aren't exactly high fashion."

"Soccer players care about scoring goals—not high fashion," Abby answers.

I nearly cheer.

Eugene has gone to get paper cups from one of the cabinets. "Who wants lemonade? What about celery and carrot sticks?"

I get that Eugene is a health nut, but I was hoping for double-chocolate-chip cookies.

Camila insists on pouring the lemonade.

"How's it going with your group?" Gustavo asks, smoothing his sister's hair. Gustavo might be annoying, but I have to admit he's a good big brother. I shouldn't have teased him before.

I catch Antoine observing Gustavo and Camila too. Maybe he's thinking about Vincent—and how, unless his mothers have another baby someday, he'll never get to be a big brother again.

"It's going pretty good," Camila tells Gustavo. "We're sharing memories about our loved one who died." She pours lemonade into Gustavo's cup slowly, so that she won't spill. "I wish I remembered Papi better."

"I know," Gustavo says.

I'm thinking about signs. Gustavo said it was a sign when Camila knocked at the door. I don't know whether I believe in signs.

I know that when Catholics pray, they make the sign of the cross. I picture the cross on Gustavo's mother's necklace. Maybe if you're religious, or if your parents are religious, it's easier to believe in signs.

That reminds me of a conversation my dad and I once had. Though we used to talk a lot, it's hard for me to remember any one conversation. More just how it felt to talk to him. Comfortable. When we were talking, I felt like there was no place else I wanted to be. Since he died, I haven't had that feeling with anyone else.

Last Father's Day, Mom suggested that Dad and I bike up to the cemetery on Mount Royal, where my grandpa is buried. "That would be the best present you could give him," Mom told me when Dad was out of earshot. I wish I'd known it would be our last Father's Day together.

Dad had bought a bouquet of daisies, and he packed them in his satchel so we could leave them on Grandpa's grave. Though the daisies were wrapped in cellophane, some of the petals started falling off. I was biking behind Dad, and I remember thinking how the petals looked like snowflakes.

The road to the cemetery is steep, so we'd stopped to stretch. We'd left our bicycles in the bushes by the road and were standing side by side, stretching our calves. "We even have the same calves," Dad said, and I remember how that made me feel proud. All my life, I've wanted to be like him.

That was when Dad started talking about my grandfather. Grandpa died before I was born, so until then, all I'd known about him was that he loved chess too. There was a black-and-white photo of Grandpa in Dad's man cave. In the photo, Grandpa looked stern. I knew without asking that he must have been a strict father.

Dad told me how Grandpa had had a drinking problem when Dad was a kid and when he was drunk he got mean, but that he'd sobered up at the end of his life. I asked Dad if that was why he never drank—not even at parties—and he said yeah, that was why. I was too shy to ask what kinds of things Grandpa did when he got mean. My dad didn't usually talk to me about that kind of personal stuff, and I think I was afraid to break the spell.

"Not long before he died," Dad said, "he told me he was sorry and asked for my forgiveness. I told him not to worry, that I'd forgiven him ages ago, but you know what, Christopher? I lied. I never really forgave him. And I wonder if he felt that all along."

It's a weird thing to recall, but I remember that at that moment Dad flicked a fly off his arm.

My dad told me Grandpa asked if he believed in life after death. "I told him I didn't know, but that I didn't think so. And then he told me, 'If there is life after death, I'll try to give you a sign from the other side.'"

So I asked my dad if Grandpa had ever given him a sign. "I'm not sure," Dad told me. "But once, not long after you were born, I had a dream that I saw him riding on a bus"—Dad's voice got hoarse at this part—"and he waved at me. I wondered if maybe that was him trying to give me a sign."

We were getting back on our bikes when I tapped my dad's elbow. "If anything ever happens to you"—I didn't use the word *die* because I didn't want to imagine a world without my dad in it—"can you give me a sign?"

Dad punched my arm. "How 'bout I wave at you from a bus?"

Just then we heard the *rat-a-tat-tat* of a woodpecker somewhere high above us. We looked up at the fir trees, searching for the woodpecker. I spotted the bird's bright red head. "There he is," I told Dad. "See? Up there, to the left."

"Hey", Dad said, "if I don't wave at you from a bus, how 'bout I send a woodpecker to let you know I'm doing okay? That I found peace."

I punched Dad's arm back.

If only I had paid more attention when Dad said *That I found peace*. Was he trying to tell me he was unhappy? And if he was, couldn't I have found a way to help him?

Camila's voice brings me back to the classroom. "Chris-to-pher, you look like you went to the moon. How much lemonade do you want?"

I hold out my cup. "Fill 'er up, *hermanita!*"

I'm suddenly thirsty. The lemonade tastes bitter and sweet at the same time.

My dad *died*—there, I said it! In nearly two years, I've never seen him in my dreams. And I haven't heard another woodpecker.

NINE

Abby

Why am I not surprised that Eugene think it's unhealthy for kids to spend a whole day cooped up inside?

"Personally," he says, flipping his wrist to show off his Fitbit, "I try to get in at least ten thousand steps a day. That comes to five miles, which meets the Centers for Disease Control's recommendation."

I nearly ask Eugene how many miles he got in when he was living on the streets. Ever notice how you never see a homeless person wearing a Fitbit?

"It's especially unhealthy to spend a whole day indoors in May, when there's not a cloud in the sky," Eugene is saying.

I look out the window. He's right. There isn't a single cloud. I used to love being outside. Lying on the grass on warm days, watching for butterflies and staring up at the clouds, or in winter, catching snowflakes on my tongue.

But now I realize this is the first time I've paid any attention to nature since…well, since Mom died.

When did the grass get so green? When did the dandelions pop up? How could I have missed all that?

"I thought we'd break up the day with a twenty-minute silent walk outside," Eugene is saying.

"Excuse me, but did you just say *silent*?" Gustavo asks. "Because we didn't do that last year or the year before." Something tells me Gustavo isn't any better with change than he is with silence.

Eugene claps Gustavo's shoulder. "You know me—I like to keep things fresh."

Gustavo gulps. "*Total* silence? As in no talking at all?"

Eugene nods. "That's the plan, my man."

Antoine says, "My maman meditates for twenty minutes every morning, So Mom and I try to stay quiet too. I used to hate it, but you get used to it."

I'm not exactly looking forward to twenty minutes of silence myself. My house has been so quiet in the last seven weeks, it's spooky. I may not be enjoying grief retreat, but I think all the noise…well…that part's okay.

The five of us follow Eugene downstairs. He checks his Fitbit. I guess he's hoping to get in an extra thousand steps. "We've been doing a lot of talking and getting to know each other this morning," he explains, "so the point of this exercise is to give our minds a rest and let us tune in to ourselves. It's interesting that Antoine mentioned meditation because some people call what we're about to do a walking meditation.

"I'll raise my arm to signal when the twenty minutes start, and I'll raise it again when time's up. At first, you might find it hard to stay quiet," Eugene explains.

Personally, I'm worried Gustavo might explode. I doubt that kid has ever been quiet for twenty minutes straight. Not during waking hours anyway.

"Anyone need to make a pit stop in the bathroom before we head out?" Eugene asks, "or is it just me?"

None of us need to use the bathroom, so we wait outside for Eugene. Felicia and I sit on a stone bench by the entrance to the school. The boys check out a black convertible parked at the corner. I can hear them talking about cars and video games.

"Why do you think he hates you?" I ask Felicia, lifting my eyes toward Christopher.

"No idea," she says, tapping one sandal on the ground. I guess she doesn't want to discuss it, because she changes the topic. "Aren't you worried you're going to ruin your precious cleats? Shouldn't you keep them for the soccer pitch? Do you even *have* a pretty pair of sandals?" She lifts one foot in the air and flexes her foot to show off her shoe.

"I'm not the pretty-sandal type. Besides, my dad'll buy me another pair of cleats."

"Wouldn't that be a waste of money?" Felicia asks.

"Maybe."

Felicia changes the topic again. "So what do you think of grief retreat so far?"

"To be honest, I already got all the help I needed from Mrs. Goldfarb. She told me to get on with life. *Look forward, not backward*," I say in my best imitation of Mrs. Goldfarb.

"Isn't there anything at all you like about it?" Felicia asks.

"Well, I like meeting you—and the other kids. Till this morning, I don't think I ever met another kid who had a parent who died...or two parents."

Felicia flexes her foot again. Even her toenails are painted black. "You know what my favorite part is? The stories," she says. "I can't get over how—" She doesn't finish her sentence. She is probably about to change the topic again. Maybe she has ADD. She's like a bird that hops from branch to branch, looking for the right spot to settle—but never quite finding it. "Can you believe Eugene lived on the streets? Or that Gustavo's father never even tried a cigarette—but that he still got lung cancer? Or that Antoine's mothers—it must be *so* weird having two mothers—found their baby dead in his crib? Talk about unfair!"

I shrug. "Life's unfair. It's unfair that my mom caught a virus that weakened her heart. And it's unfair that she didn't get a new heart in time. And it's unfair that you lost both of your parents..."

Felicia sighs. Maybe I shouldn't have mentioned that. But it turns out that's not why she sighed. "Do you think we'll *ever* find out what happened to Christopher's father? Not knowing is *killing* me. Oops!" she says, covering her mouth.

I wave my hand to let her know it's okay. "I think Christopher's dad died on the job," I say. "I bet he was doing something heroic."

"You mean like pulling someone out of the path of a moving train and then getting hit by the train? Or intervening in a knife attack and then getting knifed by the perp?" Felicia asks.

"You're really good at making stuff up, aren't you?"

Felicia grins. "Let's just say I have an extremely active imagination. My media-studies teacher says filmmakers—even documentary filmmakers—need imagination."

"Hey, weren't we just talking about Christopher's dad?"

"You're right. I get carried away sometimes."

"You can say that again. But hey, I still really like talking to you." I don't want Felicia to think I'm criticizing her.

"Me too. Anyway"—she lowers her voice as if she's about to let me in on a secret—"I don't think Christopher's dad was doing something heroic."

"Why not?"

"Because he'd have told us about it. Who wouldn't tell if his dad was a hero?"

"Hmm," I say. "Good point."

The door to the school swings open, and Eugene comes out. He raises his arm the way he said he would to signal the start of the exercise. Felicia and I exchange a nod as we get up from the bench. The boys are still admiring the car. I hear Christopher say he thinks it has something called an intelligent parking assist system. Gustavo says his mom could use a car like that.

"Christoph—" I call out, but then I realize I just broke the silence. I didn't even make it for three seconds. How will I last another nineteen minutes and fifty-seven seconds?

The boys fall into step behind us.

I keep thinking of other things I want to talk to Felicia about. After her parents died, did she stop noticing the sky too? Did she ever try playing soccer? What neighborhood do she and her grandparents live in? If we live close enough, we could get together and go for walks. Noisy ones.

We loop around the school, and then Eugene leads us up a side street. Once or twice he turns to check on us, as if he's worried one of us might try to escape. The street is steep. We could head back down, but Eugene must think we need an aerobic workout.

Not talking feels weird. Especially when a woman comes out of her house carrying a tin watering can and calls out, "Good morning!" Eugene waves, but the rest of us don't say a word. The woman gives us a strange look. Maybe she thinks we're mutes.

Felicia winks at me. I try winking back, though I'm a terrible winker. Maybe I can ask Felicia for a lesson.

"Watch ou—" I hear Gustavo start to say behind me. Felicia and I spin around and see that Christopher's shoe-lace has come untied. Antoine grabs Christopher's arm so he doesn't trip.

Christopher reties the lace. Eugene nods approvingly. Gustavo opens his mouth to say something, but Eugene slides one finger over his mouth, zipping his lips.

How many minutes of silence are left? I try concentrating on my breathing and my posture. Our soccer coach says good posture is a soccer player's best friend. After I do that for a while, I count the cracks in the sidewalk, and then I stare at Felicia's glossy black toenails. I've never worn toenail polish. And fingernail polish only once or twice. I don't see the point of it.

I step a little to the right so I won't squash a fat ant coming my way. The ant is carrying a chunk of bread that is bigger than he is.

There is something comforting about the sounds of our footsteps as we trudge back toward the school. The air smells like bacon. Someone is making a late breakfast. I don't know when it happened, but it is getting easier to walk in silence.

A girl comes toward us on a skateboard. So what if she thinks we're mutes?

The girl stops in her tracks. "Jessie Towers!" she says, looking right at Felicia. "What's up? I've been following you on Instagram. I love your pics—and your comments are so wicked! They crack me up!"

Felicia shrugs, then shakes her head and turns her hands palm side up. She is using gestures to tell the girl she has mistaken her for someone else.

The girl jumps back on her skateboard. "Weird!" she says as she takes off along Sherbrooke Street.

TEN

Christopher

"Who's Jessie Towers?" I ask Felicia. Now that silent meditation is over, I can finally ask.

Keeping quiet for twenty minutes wasn't as hard for me as it was for the other kids. Chess players stay quiet a lot. We study the board while we plan our next moves—and try to figure out our opponent's strategy. I prefer quiet. I hate when people talk for the sake of talking the way Gustavo does. I also hate chitchat and gossip.

I wonder what Felicia's next move will be.

She rolls her eyes. "How should I know?" Then she meets my gaze—I decide that would be hard for me to do if I was lying—and adds, "I guess Jessie Towers looks like me. Lucky girl!" She tosses back her hair and giggles.

I'm about to say I haven't seen many thirteen-year-olds with bleached hair and heavy eye makeup when Eugene interrupts. "People are always asking if I'm George Clooney."

"Hey, did you just make a joke?" Abby asks him.

"Eugene has a very good sense of humor," Gustavo chimes in.

"It wasn't a joke," Eugene says, adjusting his comb-over. "They say I have George's hair. Sort of." Eugene stops at the water fountain and takes a long, noisy gulp of water.

"George Clooney doesn't slurp," Abby calls out.

Though it isn't that hot outside or in the school, Eugene can't stop sweating. Even after he mops his face with his handkerchief, he starts sweating again.

"So, George Clooney, you feeling all right?" I ask. "Any nausea or chest pain?"

"I'm good." Eugene taps his chest with one hand. "But thanks for asking. You already sound like a paramedic, Christopher."

I don't think I've ever had a better compliment. What I didn't tell the others is that my dad was part of our province's elite advanced-care paramedic squad. That meant he could administer certain meds and use equipment regular paramedics aren't allowed to. It also meant my dad got called in to work the really tough cases.

One day I'm going to join the elite advanced-care squad too. But just as I think that, a new thought crosses my mind. If my dad hadn't been part of the elite squad, if he hadn't had to handle the worst cases, he might not have gotten PTSD. And he might still be alive.

If only there was a way to turn back the clock. If only I could have got my dad the help he needed. I was his son.

Isn't a son supposed to know his dad better than almost anyone else?

We're all thirsty. I end up last in line for the water fountain, probably because I've been thinking about Dad and the elite advanced-care squad and what I wish I'd done differently.

I could have predicted Eugene would want to discuss the silent-meditation exercise, though I figured he would at least wait till we were back upstairs. But Eugene can't wait. "So how did the silent walk work out for you people?" he asks when we are still in line at the fountain.

Gustavo is leaning over the spout, drinking water, but that doesn't stop him from talking. "It was hard, like you said," he manages to say. "But then it got..." I can't make out the rest. When Gustavo steps away from the fountain, he has so much water in his mouth that his cheeks look like a chipmunk's.

"It wasn't a total disaster," Abby says. "I noticed things I usually wouldn't. Like this ant I nearly stepped on."

Gustavo wipes the water from his lips. "I saw him too. He was carrying a chunk of bread, right? Did you know ants can carry fifty times their body weight?"

I nudge Gustavo. "I liked you better when you were silent."

"S-orr-y," Gustavo stammers, and I have to explain I'm only kidding.

"I'm guessing it wasn't too hard for you, Antoine, since you told us how you're used to quiet time at home," Eugene says.

"Kind of," Antoine says. "Except it was hard when we passed this old Mercedes, and I wanted to make sure the other guys saw it too."

"The silver one at the corner of Montrose?" I say.

Eugene still wants to know what Felicia and I thought of the exercise.

"I'm good with silence," I tell him.

"We noticed that," Felicia says.

I don't react. Felicia is trying to push me into talking about how my dad died. But I'm still not ready to do that. I don't know if I'll ever be.

"I didn't like the exercise," Felicia says. "I kept wanting to talk to Abby." She squeezes Abby's hand.

Sheesh! It hasn't taken those two long to become BFFs. All that hand squeezing makes me glad I'm not a girl.

There is something else I'm wondering about. Am I the only one at grief retreat who is suspicious of Felicia?

So, as if I were playing chess, I plan my strategy.

I try saying, "Hey, Jessie…"

If Felicia turns around, I'll know she has something to hide.

Felicia doesn't turn around.

But the muscles in her neck twitch.

Check, I think to myself. Not checkmate. But definitely check.

ELEVEN

Abby

You know how Eugene said some people get stuck in a certain feeling after someone they love has died? At the time, I didn't think much of his theory. But when Eugene starts to explain this feeling—he calls it *could have, would have, should have* and *what if*—I decide maybe he was right, because I think that's where I could be stuck.

And I can't imagine ever getting unstuck.

We are back upstairs after the silent walk. Lunch is in half an hour, so Eugene thinks it's a good time to explain more stuff. He is using the whiteboard, and when he writes those eight words, I suddenly think about how, BMGS (my abbreviation for Before Mom Got Sick), she used to love going to flea markets and hunting for antiques. One time, Mom fell in love with a lamp made from an old maple-syrup jug. When she told Dad she'd paid a hundred and fifty dollars for it, I remember him saying she *should have* tried to get a better price. But then Mom told Dad she didn't have the *heart* to haggle with the woman who sold it to her. I remember her telling Dad, "So what if I paid a few dollars more? The vendors have to make a living, don't they? Besides, I don't believe in should haves."

Now Eugene underlines *could have, would have, should have* and *what if* twice.

That's when I realize that in this way, at least, I take after my dad. Because I think those words all the time. They *should have* named me Abby "*Could Have*" Lefebvre.

Could Mom *have* fought off the virus that weakened her heart?

Could Mom's immune system *have* been stronger?

Could Mom's name *have* come up on the transplant list sooner?

Should Mom *have* gotten more bed rest? That was what Dr. Burton recommended, but Mom hated staying in bed all day. She'd insist on seeing me off in the morning when I left for school, and when I let myself back in at a quarter to four, she'd get out of bed again and come and sit with me on the couch so she could hear about my day. Our house has a lot of stairs. Maybe if Mom *could have* stayed in bed and not had to go up and down so many stairs, she *would have* been stronger—and she *would have* lived long enough to get a new heart.

What if we'd lived in a house with fewer stairs?

The thing about *could have, would have, should have* and *what if* conversations is they never end. They're like rabbits—you start with two and you end up with two thousand.

It turns out we're all obsessed with *could have, would have, should have* and *what if.*

Antoine goes first. "I wonder," he says, "if I *should have* gone in to check on Vincent the night he died. If I'd noticed he wasn't breathing, then maybe the paramedics *could have* saved him."

"*What if* my papi had come to Canada when he was a kid?" Gustavo adds. "He grew up in the Norte Grande part of Chile, where there are many copper mines. Even if we don't know for sure that exposure to copper dust causes lung cancer, it is possible. But then I think how if my papi had left Chile when he was a kid, he would never have met my mami, and I would never have been born. Or Camila either." Gustavo's voice, which was sad to begin with, gets even sadder when he imagines Camila never having been born.

"Those are great examples of *could haves* and *what ifs,*" Eugene says. "After someone we love dies it's normal to feel vulnerable, powerless." He adds the words *vulnerable* and *powerless* to the whiteboard. "We have the sense that death can strike at any time. Saying *could have, would have, should have* and *what if* gives us a feeling of power," he says.

Christopher shrugs. "Power? I don't get it. I think I *should have* been there to help my father. That doesn't make me feel powerful. It makes me feel power*less.*"

I shoot Felicia a look. I think we're all still surprised any time Christopher contributes to a conversation without being forced to.

Felicia winks at me.

"I see why you're confused," Eugene tells Christopher, "so let me backtrack. By thinking *I should have been there to help my father*, what you're really saying is, *I would have been able to change the outcome*." Eugene chooses his words carefully. That's when I realize he knows whatever it is that Christopher doesn't want to tell the rest of us.

"I *should have* been able to help him," Christopher says, but then he stops and corrects himself. "I *could have* changed the outcome."

When Eugene speaks, his voice is a mix of calm and sad. "All the *could haves*, *should haves*, *would haves* and *what ifs* in the world can't change what's already happened. If you knew what was going to happen, Christopher, you might have made some different decisions. But at the moment you were in, you made the best decisions you could. The reason we beat ourselves up so much is that we're looking at situations in hindsight."

Antoine nods. I imagine he's still thinking about Vincent.

I can see Felicia's eyes darting from Eugene to Christopher. I bet she wants Christopher to tell us more. I'm curious too, but I also have this weird urge to protect him. No one should force anyone to share their story. I like Felicia. She's cool and fun, but even if I haven't known her long, I know she's used to getting her way and she sometimes blurts out stuff she shouldn't say—like her comments about my soccer shorts and cleats. So before she can start prodding Christopher with questions, I jump in with my own *could haves, would haves, should haves* and *what ifs*.

Let me make this clear: I'm not participating because I think it'll help *me*. Only because I want to help Christopher.

I explain about the virus, the waiting list for the heart transplant, how Mom *could have* gotten more bed rest—even about the stairs in our house. "Sometimes I can't sleep because I don't know how to turn off the *could have, would have, should have* and *what if* switch."

"You've taken the first step, Abby," Eugene says, "just by talking about it."

I shake my head. Telling the others about my *could haves* only makes me feel worse. This is why I should never have come to grief retreat.

Felicia sniffles, then wipes the bottom of her nose. "I wonder what *would have* happened if we hadn't gone up to our chalet that weekend. And what *would have* happened if the temperature had been lower and the lake's surface was completely frozen."

I can see Felicia is fighting tears, so I pat her back. She's gone through so much, and she's so brave!

"Though this might be hard for you kids to imagine," Eugene says, "the *could haves, would haves, should haves* and *what ifs* eventually stop. There's no schedule though. Eventually you'll be able to move from what *what if* to *what is*.

There aren't too many things in life we can control. And we can't change the past."

"What about guilt?" I didn't plan to ask the question. It just pops out.

Antoine sighs. Christopher straightens his neck and shoulders. Felicia doesn't react at all.

"Guilt is another feeling that often comes up during the grieving process," Eugene says. "Is there something you want to tell us about feeling guilty, Abby?"

"Me?" I say. "No. I was just wondering is all."

There's a little voice talking to me in the back of my head. I keep speaking because I want to drown out the sound. "Maybe," I say, "we feel guilty that we didn't do more, that we couldn't save our parents—or our sibling." I make sure not to look at anyone when I say that.

Eugene nods slowly. Why do I keep getting the feeling he knows what I'm thinking? "There's no use in my telling any of you not to feel guilty," he says. "But I will tell you it's better not to pursue that guilt. Like I said before, we all made the best decisions we could at the time we made them. If any of you ever feel guilty, it helps to remind yourself of that."

The little voice won't be stilled. It is saying, "*You* had the virus first. *You* gave your mom the virus that killed her."

TWELVE

Christopher

I might need another silent walk.

No one warned me grief retreat would be this hard.

All that talking about the stuff we *could have, should have* and *would have* done stirred me up inside. Abby isn't the only one who lies in bed at night thinking about those things. I do too. And I really wish Abby hadn't mentioned guilt. Eugene is right—we need to move from *what if* to *what is*. If only he could show us how to do it. Sometimes I feel like I'm standing at the water's edge. I see the shore on the other side, but I don't know how to reach it. There's no bridge, and it's too far to swim.

When I lose at chess—it doesn't happen often—I also think *could have, should have, would have* and *what if*. I *could have* got my king to the other side of the board. I *should have* realized my opponent could take out my knight with his queen. But chess has rules. A castle can

PLANET GRIEF

only move in a straight line. A bishop cannot jump over the other pieces.

Real life doesn't have rules.

People don't always do what we want them to.

I wasn't there for my dad. I *should have* known he needed help.

I don't think that guilt will ever go away.

Besides, my dad *should have* known better. He *should have* known I'd end up feeling this way. He *shouldn't have* done that to me. He *should never have* done what he did. What kind of father would do that to his son—and his wife? I suddenly realize I am clenching my fists. When I try relaxing them, they automatically ball up again. Is it possible to be obsessed with *should have*, *could have*, *would have* and *what if* and be angry all at the same time? Eugene said different feelings can overlap. I'm so confused, my head hurts. I'm tired too. I yawn, which leads to another longer yawn. Gustavo starts yawning too. It's one way to stop him from talking.

Thank goodness we're breaking for lunch. I'm starving, but mostly I think I need a break from talking about feelings. Usually I keep my feelings inside of me, where they are safe.

We eat in the butterfly garden behind the school. There are benches and picnic tables, and Eugene says we don't have to stay with our groups. That's good news, because I'm still uncomfortable around Felicia. When Eugene announced it was time for lunch, all she wanted to know was whether she could have her phone back. Eugene said sure, we all could—so long as we put them back on the table when we get back to the classroom.

When I look over at Felicia now, she is playing with her cell. Why do I keep getting the feeling she's up to something?

There is a buffet table with a starched white tablecloth and a pot of tulips on either end. I see salads and platters of cheese and sliced meats and a basket with bagels. The desserts are out too—brownies, cookies and fruit kebabs.

A woman wearing a white apron is handing out plates, cutlery and napkins. "*Bon appétit*," she says as she hands me a plate. Her name tag says *Gretchen*, and underneath, in smaller letters, it says *Volunteer, Montreal Funeral Services*. The word *funeral* makes my shoulders tense up.

Even though all Gretchen has said to me is *bon appétit*, I know she feels sorry for me—for all of us grieving kids. And that bothers me. I hate the idea of some stranger feeling sorry for me.

Abby is reading the tag on Gretchen's apron too. "Montreal Funeral Services?" Abby says. "You advertising for customers?"

I can't believe Abby just said that. When I laugh, I spill some of the Greek salad I just put on my plate.

Gretchen grabs some napkins to mop up the mess. "Not advertising," she says. "Just trying to be useful."

"Want me to throw those out for you?" Antoine offers, pointing to the wet napkins Gretchen has left on a corner of the buffet table.

"Yes," she says, "And thank you, young man."

Gustavo wants to know if there is mayo in the coleslaw. "Mayonnaise goes bad quickly in warm weather," he tells Gretchen. "It's one of the most common causes of severe food poisoning."

"I just took the coleslaw out of the fridge," Gretchen assures him, but she looks a little concerned.

"I guess you don't want to kill any of the kids who come to grief retreat," Abby says. "Though a severe case or two of food poisoning could mean extra business for Montreal Funeral Services."

This time, even Gretchen chuckles.

Felicia helps herself to a giant serving of coleslaw. "This coleslaw smells delicious," I hear her tell Gretchen. "If you don't mind my asking, is there some reason you volunteer at grief retreat? Is it because you lost someone you loved when you were a kid?"

Gretchen leans in to answer Felicia's question, but I move away from the buffet table as quickly as possible. I need a break from sad stories.

The parents and the younger kids are streaming into the butterfly garden. I spot my mom talking to Abby's dad and Antoine's maman. Gustavo's mami and Camila are behind them. When Camila sees Gustavo, she lets go of her mami's hand and rushes over to us.

Camila grabs on to Gustavo's knees and hugs him. Gustavo doesn't seem to mind that he has been immobilized.

"Are you and Gustavo best friends?" Camila asks me. "Or do you think he talks too much?"

"He does talk too much, but we're friends," I tell Camila. "Not exactly best friends though."

Camila nods as if this is promising news. Then she turns to Antoine. "What about you? Can you be Gustavo's best friend?"

"Maybe," Antoine says. "We both like video games and nice cars."

My mom taps my shoulder. "How are you finding it so far?" she whispers.

"It's pretty intense," I tell her. "What about you? How's the parents' workshop? How are you holding up?" What I really want to know is whether she's told the others about how Dad died. But I can't ask that—not with so many other people milling around.

"I'm holding up fine. It feels good to be here," my mother says. "It helps to feel supported." The way she says it makes me think she has told the others. What if they go home tonight and tell their kids?

Maybe I can talk her into letting me stay home tomorrow.

"Don't feel you have to sit with me at lunch," she says. "You should go ahead and be with your friends."

"You sure you're okay without me? I'll sit with you if you need me to."

I notice Mom exchange a look with Abby's dad and Antoine's maman. When she says, "You don't need to worry about me all the time, Christopher," I know for sure she's been talking about me.

Camila can't decide if she should sit with her mami at the adult table or with me and Gustavo. So she ends up flitting between the two tables—another butterfly in the garden—until her mami makes her sit down beside her.

Antoine and his maman excuse themselves to make a call. "To check on my mom," Antoine explains.

Gustavo gets up and leaves the butterfly garden—I guess he needs to use the bathroom. I'm glad to be able to sit quietly for a bit. There are many plants in the butterfly garden, but only the tulips and daffodils are blooming. Two white butterflies flit by. I watch them disappear over the fence.

"¿Donde esta mi hermano?"

Camila is tugging on my pants. When I look down at her, I see that her dark eyes are shiny with tears. "Where'd he go?" she asks, in English this time. Her hands are shaking.

Her mother rushes over to my table. "What's wrong, mi amor?" Eugene comes jogging over too.

"I don't know wh-where Gus-Gustavo went." It sounds like she's hyperventilating.

"Don't worry," I tell Camila. "He just went to the bathroom."

"I was just in the bathroom," Eugene says. "I didn't see him. Maybe he was in one of the stalls."

Camila wails. The sound reminds me of the siren we heard before. Even when her mother picks her up, Camila doesn't stop. She kicks her legs and calls for Gustavo.

She is not behaving like a regular kid.

Then I catch myself.

Camila is not a regular kid.

Regular kids are not three years old when their dads die.

I stroke Camila's hair the way I saw Gustavo do before.

Ever since my dad died, I've felt like I have it worse than anybody else. But maybe there are other kids who have it just as bad. Or even worse.

THIRTEEN

Abby

I've never seen anyone freak out like that. Camila was bawling and kicking and screaming for Gustavo. Nobody could console her. Not her mami and not Eugene, and he's her hero.

Felicia says it was a panic attack. I'm not so sure. A boy in my class had a panic attack, and he couldn't get a word out. Camila never stopped screaming.

Gustavo was only gone five minutes. He went to put the coleslaw in the refrigerator. That kid worries about everything, including salmonella.

When Camila saw Gustavo walking back into the butterfly garden, she let out such a squeal you'd think he'd returned from the dead. *Returned from the dead.* When those words go through my head I suddenly understand what Camila was afraid of—that Gustavo was dead. Why else would she freak out like that?

Felicia and I watched the whole thing from our picnic table. I was about to look for Gustavo myself, but Felicia wasn't too concerned. "He'll turn up," she said. "And she'll stop shrieking. She'll burst my eardrum if she keeps carrying on like that."

When we go back to the buffet for seconds, she says, "If I could only eat one thing for the rest of my life it would be lettuce."

"Me too," I tell her. "With blue-cheese dressing."

Felicia looks at me like I just said something incredible. "Blue cheese is my favorite dressing too! Not a lot of kids like blue-cheese dressing."

When we are back at the picnic table, I tell Felicia my theory about Camila. "You know how grown-ups always say stuff like *death happens* and *death is part of life*? You can't argue with those things because they're true. Death happens, and sure, it's part of life. One morning you find your goldfish belly-up in his bowl. Your great-granduncle dies at the old folks' home.

"But when you're a kid and one of your parents dies, death isn't far away anymore. I bet that's why Camila freaked out. She was worried Gustavo was dead."

Felicia is watching my face. Something interesting is going through her head. "That's totally poetic," she says. "Especially the part about the goldfish. Hey, Abby, can I ask you something?"

"Sure. Ask away." I'm hoping Felicia will say something about getting together after the weekend.

"Would you mind saying what you just said on video?"

"Video? Why would I want to do that?"

Felicia takes her cell phone out of her pocket and lays it flat on her lap. "To help me. I was thinking"—Felicia pauses—"maybe I could make a short documentary about this grief retreat."

I've been leaning over the picnic table to talk to Felicia, but now I lean away from her. "About grief retreat? I thought we swore to keep things confidential."

"That's why I'm asking your permission."

"I need to think about it. Who'd see this documentary?"

"I haven't figured that out yet. Hopefully, as many people as possible. Here's the thing—there's a short-doc contest for Montreal-area high-school students. My media-studies teacher thought I should submit something. I so want to wi—" Felicia stops herself in midsentence. "A documentary like that could end up helping a lot of people. That's why I want to make it, of course. To help others. Totally. Not for myself."

Felicia has a point. But I'm still not sure I want to be in a documentary. "All I have to do is say that stuff about the goldfish? Would I have to talk about my mom?"

"Not if you don't want to. But it would add *context*. My teacher says context is really important in a documentary."

"Is that why you've been taking notes?" For the first time since I met Felicia, I wonder if she's been acting so friendly because she wants me to be part of her project.

"Uh, no," she says. The fact that she doesn't look at me makes me wonder if she's telling the truth. "Well, yes and no."

"Put your cell phone away," I tell Felicia. I wait for her to put it back in her pocket. "Like I told you, I'll think about it."

Felicia sighs. As I mentioned, she's used to getting her way.

"One more thing," I say to Felicia. "Do you really like blue-cheese dressing?"

Felicia rolls her eyes. "Why are you even asking me that?"

At the other end of the butterfly garden, Camila is still glommed on to her brother. She is curled up next to him on the picnic bench the way Jupiter curls up with me when I'm reading on the sofa. I wouldn't be surprised to hear Camila purring.

Antoine and his maman are finally eating. I overheard them on the phone before, checking on Antoine's mom. They asked whether she had eaten anything yet today. Antoine didn't say which one of his mothers gave birth to Vincent. I'd tell all this to Felicia—except now I worry she might want to use it in her documentary. Because I'm starting to wonder if Felicia cares more about stories than the people in them.

Gustavo and Camila's mom is back at the adults' table. My dad is sitting across from her. He is watching Camila too, and he's smiling. It's been a while since I saw him smile.

He says something to Camila's mom, and she throws her head back and laughs. Is it possible my dad said something funny?

Nah, impossible.

I can feel Felicia watching me watching my dad. "I think he likes her," she says.

"Who wouldn't like Camila? She's adorable—even if she shrieks when she's upset. She's funny too. Even if it's not on purpose."

"I wasn't talking about Camila. I was talking about Camila's mom. She's lively, and I think your dad likes her. Look how he's stroking his chin when he talks to her. That's a sign."

"No way," I say. "That's gross. Besides, my dad's not like that."

"Not like what?" Felicia asks.

"He wouldn't be interested in another woman. My mom just died."

I wish Felicia hadn't said that. It isn't right. My dad may be a doofus, he may get on my nerves, but I'm not ready for him to have a girlfriend. And I'm definitely not ready for a stepmother. Even worse, I'd have Gustavo for a stepbrother. I'd never get a moment's peace.

"It's what grown-ups do," Felicia says, making it sound as if she is an expert on all grown-up behavior. "They fall in love. When they do, they forget all about the person they were with before."

FOURTEEN

Christopher

I never thought I'd say this, but Gustavo could be growing on me. Yes, he's a motormouth know-it-all worrywart (who ever heard of mayonnaise going bad in thirty minutes?), but his heart is in the right place. (I better not say that around Abby.) I know he's good-hearted because of how he treats Camila. When she freaked out, I'd have gotten annoyed and told her she was overreacting, but Gustavo didn't do that. Instead he apologized to Camila for making her worry and promised he'd always be there for her.

Did my dad ever make me that promise?

Because if he did, he broke it.

I'm not looking forward to discussing what Eugene wrote on the board before we broke for lunch. Because it's the thing that killed my dad.

When I was growing up and Dad got in from an overnight shift, he'd come to sit with me and Mom in the kitchen.

He'd rub his eyes and yawn, but I guess hanging out with us helped him chill out. He'd talk about the people he'd met on his shift. They were mostly funny stories or else stories with happy endings. Like the time some guy called 9-1-1 and said he was having a medical crisis, only it turned out his computer had frozen. Dad and his partner could have reported the guy, but they ended up fixing his computer. *It was a slow night anyhow*, Dad told us.

Then there was the lady who gave birth to twins on the sidewalk outside her house. Dad delivered the babies and cut the umbilical cords. The lady promised to name one Christopher—after my dad. Which means there's another Christopher besides me named for him. That other Christopher is probably seven or eight by now. I wonder what kind of kid he turned out to be. I'm glad he doesn't know what happened to the man he was named after.

Dad must have had sad stories too—stories about people he couldn't save—but he never told us those in the kitchen. Or else maybe he told Mom after I left for school.

I don't know exactly when things changed, only that in the last few years when Dad got in from his shift, he'd go straight to his man cave in the basement. There were times he didn't even bother saying hello to us. Sometimes we'd hear him watching TV—usually comedies with loud laugh tracks or history shows with serious-sounding narrators and dramatic music. Other times, there'd be no noise at all.

Once I asked Mom if she thought it would be okay if I asked Dad if he wanted company, but she shook her head and told me it was better to leave him be. That he needed alone time. *That's how he decompresses*, she said. I didn't want to remind her that he used to decompress by hanging out with us.

Since the day of Dad's death, I haven't been down to the basement. Not even once.

So I am kind of relieved when we get back to the classroom after lunch and Eugene explains that we'll be spending the rest of today on another art activity. My heart sinks when he says, "I'll work in some more information as we go along." I am going to have to learn about the last thing he wrote on the board after all: *the deep sadness of grief.*

This art activity has two parts, and we're doing the first part today. If I can talk my mom into letting me stay home tomorrow, I can avoid part two.

Gustavo spreads newspapers out on the table. Eugene unloads more art supplies from a metal cabinet—acrylic paint, paintbrushes, scissors, white glue and a pile of old magazines.

Antoine predicts we're making a collage.

"Guess again!" Eugene says. Now he pulls out a pile of gray cardboard masks from under the table.

"We're making grief masks," Gustavo says. There he goes, showing off his inside knowledge again. Just when I thought maybe I liked him.

"What's a grief mask?" Antoine asks.

Eugene sits down at the head of the table. He grabs one mask from the pile, flipping it over to show us both sides. "We all wear masks," he says.

"Well, bank robbers do," Abby says. "And trick-or-treaters."

Eugene tugs at the elastic band on the back of the mask and lets it snap back into place. "I mean another kind of mask. A more personal mask. The masks we wear around others. The masks that keep us safe."

"So what you're saying is, we're all a bunch of phonies?" Abby asks.

Felicia thinks that's funny.

Eugene doesn't respond right away. He's treating Abby's question like it wasn't a joke. "No, not really. It means we're all a little afraid to let our true feelings show."

That makes me think about my dad decompressing in the basement. Was he afraid to let his feelings show? What kind of mask did he wear around other people? And what about me? Do I wear a mask? I rub my cheeks, half expecting to feel cardboard there.

"This afternoon we're going to recreate our outside masks." Eugene runs his fingers over the surface of the mask, over the grooves where the eyelids go and around the nose. "You can use any materials you want to decorate your mask. You can paint or use felt pens or do collage."

"I told you it was collage," Antoine says.

"The goal is to create a version of the mask you wear when you're with others."

"What if we're bad at art?" Gustavo asks. Judging by the bicycle he drew this morning, he must be talking about himself.

"We can all make art," Eugene says. "I don't want you to worry about whether what you make is good or terrible. All that matters is that it's true."

That's it for instructions.

Felicia grabs a mask. She uses a red felt pen to draw an oval tear under one eyehole. When she sees me watching her, she covers her mask with her hand.

Antoine is quick to get started too. He draws a basket-ball first. When he writes *NBA 2K17* next to it, I realize that playing video games is part of his outside mask.

I eye the blank mask on the table in front of me. I pick up a red felt pen, remove the cap, but then drop it back on the table.

The others are drawing or using acrylic paints. I grab a couple of magazines from the stack on the table.

They're old *Sports Illustrated* magazines. One has a swim-suit model on the cover. She's hot, but she doesn't belong on my mask.

I flip through the second *Sports Illustrated*. There's an interview with a weight-lifting champion. I stop at a photo-graph of him lifting a giant barbell. His eyes are closed, and even the muscles in his face are tensed up. I tear out the page. I also tear out an ad for free weights. The weights come from a company named Be Strong. I reach for a pair of scissors and cut out the company's name.

Eugene never said we had to use pictures on our masks. I'm more into words than pictures. So that's what I'm going to use for my mask. If I can't find the words I want, I can always find the letters and make the words that way. I look for an *I*, an *H* and a *T* on the next page.

Abby nudges me. "What are you doing—writing a ransom note?"

"Yeah," I tell her. "I've been kidnapped. I want someone to come and rescue me from Planet Grief."

"Me too," Abby says. "I heard it was a double kidnapping. Two grieving kids for the price of one."

Soon I have all the letters I need. Before I start gluing them onto my mask, I arrange them in front of me as if I were playing Scrabble.

It doesn't matter that some of the letters are capitals and others are in lowercase or that the fonts are different.

I take a deep breath as I read the message I want to use on my outside mask:

i HavE to BE STRONG

FIFTEEN

Abby

I'll tell you what makes me deeply sad.

Hearing about the deep sadness of grief.

Of course, Eugene says this is another part in the grieving process where a lot of people get stuck. "That's what happened to me. Looking back, I'd say I was deeply sad for about twenty-five years," he tells us.

"I thought you were stuck at frozen," I call out.

"I was stuck at frozen. But also at deeply sad," he says.

Antoine whistles. "Twenty-five years? That's almost twice our lifetimes."

Eugene referred to his notes when he was explaining how grieving people get obsessed with *could haves*, *would haves*, *should haves* and *what ifs*. But now he puts away his folder.

He says that for him the deep sadness of grief was like a thick fog that wouldn't lift. "When I say *thick*, I mean thick as maple syrup. I found it hard to do anything—get outta bed, wash the dishes, go to work, talk to people, even phone a friend. I didn't see the point of any of it. The deep sadness of grief can be very tiring. It can sap your energy. I put on a lot of weight during those years. Try to imagine me a hundred pounds heavier."

Yikes. That is not a pretty picture. Now I get why he's a fitness freak.

Eugene explains that not every deeply sad person gets fat. He says some deeply sad people stop eating and get dangerously thin. "The deep sadness of grief doesn't come in one-size-fits-all. There are deeply sad people who sleep all the time. Others have insomnia. They go for weeks, months even, without a decent sleep. Sometimes they resort to medication to help them sleep—that can turn into a crutch."

Christopher drops his mask when Eugene says that. "So is deep sadness the same as depression?" he asks Eugene.

I'm curious to know the answer too. Depression was one of Mrs. Goldfarb's favorite subjects. She never said anything about the deep sadness of grief.

"Not quite," Eugene tells him. "Some depression is what's known as clinical. Meaning it's not caused by a particular situation. What I'm talking about when I say the *deep sadness of grief* is a sadness that comes from missing a person, the sadness of knowing they're gone for good and your life will never, ever be the same." From the way

Eugene's voice drops, I decide that just talking about the deep sadness of grief is making him deeply sad too.

I don't like the way the contoured lips of my mask are pressed together. So I use pale-pink acrylic paint to draw new lips over the cardboard ones. I extend the lips into an oval.

Gustavo peers over my shoulder. Maybe he needs ideas for his outside mask. "Let me guess. That's you laughing, right?"

"Nope," I tell him, "it's me yawning."

When I was little, I'd doze off before Mom got to the end of whatever bedtime story she was reading to me. We used to joke that I never knew if Max in *Where the Wild Things Are* found his way home—or whether Alexander's terrible, horrible, no good, very bad day ever got better.

Now I dread getting into bed at night, because no matter how late it is, or how tired I feel, I end up lying there, staring at the ceiling. Is it possible I'm not just angry and obsessed with *what if* questions but am also deeply sad?

Antoine sucks in his breath, which means he wants to say something. "Everyone's been telling me my mom's depressed. Since Vincent died, she's been going around in pajamas all day. Maman and I have to make sure she eats— and takes a shower." Antoine bites his lip as if he's worried he's just shared a secret he shouldn't have.

"Not doing self-care—things like eating well and showering—can be another symptom of the deep sadness of grief," Eugene says.

"So maybe my mom isn't depressed. Maybe she has the deep sadness of grief." Antoine sucks in his breath again. "Does it ever go away?"

"Yup," Eugene answers. "It gets softer. Not so deep. And easier to live with." He looks Antoine in the eye. "Your mom is gonna be okay."

Antoine bites his lower lip. "Are you sure?"

"Yup."

Christopher is gluing more letters onto his mask. When he speaks, he doesn't look at any of us. It's as if he's talking to the mask. "My dad had PTSD," he says in a quiet voice without much emotion in it.

Eugene usually comments when one of us says something, but not this time. The rest of us continue working on our masks. Even Felicia doesn't try to push Christopher into telling us more.

I've heard of PTSD, but I'm not exactly sure what the letters stand for, so I'm glad when Gustavo breaks the silence. "What's PTSD anyhow?"

"Post-traumatic stress disorder," Christopher says, his voice as flat as it was before. He doesn't say anything else after that, so the words just hang in the air. *Post-traumatic stress disorder.*

Eugene gets up to change the water I used to clean my paintbrush. "Sometimes people go through things that are just too much for them to bear. That can lead to PTSD. Soldiers get it a lot. So do first responders," he says when he sits back down. "But we don't have to talk about that now."

He doesn't look at Christopher. "Unless, of course, you want to."

Christopher sighs.

When he sees I've noticed, he turns the sigh into a yawn. Then he covers his mouth and yawns some more. Obviously, Christopher doesn't want to say more about his dad's PTSD right now.

Thank god it's almost four o'clock, time for grief retreat to break up for the day. Eugene says we can leave our masks on the table or take them home. "But if you take yours home," he tells us, "make sure to bring it back tomorrow. Also, for tomorrow I want you each to bring a photo of the loved one—or loved ones—you're grieving."

"A photo?" Felicia says. "My, uh, my grandparents don't have a lot of photos. They, uh, we moved after my parents died."

Christopher is wrapping his mask in tissue paper. He must be taking his home. "You mean you don't have any photos on your cell?" he asks Felicia, raising his eyebrows.

"Uh, sure, of course I do. Good point," Felicia answers.

Our parents are waiting in the lobby. Antoine's maman is standing by the front door, holding her bus pass. She must be in a hurry to get home so she can check on her partner.

I keep an eye on Felicia to make sure she's okay. It must be hard for her to see everyone else's parents. She is kneeling by the table, taking photos of flowerpots.

She probably wants some arty shots for her documentary. I guess tulips can't object to being photographed.

My dad waves me over when he sees me. He is talking to Gustavo and Camila's mami. Camila is holding on to her mami's knee. I decide not to go over right away. I'll wait till they stop talking.

To keep myself busy, I study a bronze plaque in the lobby. It's engraved with the names of soldiers who gave their lives in the two world wars. They all went to Lawrence Academy. Each name is followed by the soldier's year of birth and death. A few were only eighteen when they died— that's just five years older than I am. I look around the lobby, up at the stained-glass windows, then down to the white tile floor. It's weird to think that those soldiers who sacrificed their lives for our country used to walk through this lobby and look up at the same stained-glass windows.

My dad is still gabbing. Who knew he had that much to say?

He catches my eye, and I shrug to let him know I'm getting impatient, that I'm ready to go.

"Abby?" he calls out, and now he gestures again for me to come over.

If you can't beat 'em, join 'em, I guess.

I don't ask him how the workshop for adults was. And Dad doesn't ask me how the kids' workshop was. Instead, he does something weirder. He leans over and kisses the side of my head. I'm so surprised, I forget to complain—or make a sarcastic crack.

"Raquel and I were thinking," Dad says, "how it might be fun if the five of us went to the barbecue-chicken joint for supper."

That's when I lose it. "Fun?" I say. I don't care that I've raised my voice and everyone in the lobby is turning to look at me. "Fun?" I am thinking about the young soldiers who died in battle. "Don't you know this is a grief retreat?"

SIXTEEN

Christopher

I grit my teeth. "I don't know why you had to tell them."

I can't remember the last time I got angry with my mom.

She is gripping the steering wheel so tightly her knuckles are white. "There's no point being at the grief retreat, Christopher, if we can't talk about what happened."

I look out the window. We are passing a row of low-rise apartment buildings. There's a man out on his balcony, strumming a guitar. "I'm not going back tomorrow."

"You should give it a chance."

"I did. And it's not for me."

Mom keeps her eyes on the road. "I thought you were making friends with the other boys—Gustavo and Antoine. They've been through a lot too. Their mothers are nice."

"Gustavo never shuts up. Antoine's obsessed with video games."

"Gustavo's sister, Camila, she stopped talking for two years after her father died. Antoine was the one who found his baby brother."

I turn to look at her. "He was? He didn't tell us that. How do you know all those things anyhow?"

"Because we *talked*, Christopher. And it helped. It helped a lot. We shared our stories."

I sigh. "Now all the kids are going to know what Dad did. And they won't look at me the same way. They're going to feel sorry for me—and I hate that. I swear, I hate that more than anything. I'm *not* going back tomorrow. No way." The mask I started is on my lap. I unwrap it from the tissue paper. Then I unroll the car window and hold the mask out so it flutters in the warm breeze. I nearly let go of it. I imagine watching it fly up into the sky like a kite. But then I change my mind and lay it back on my lap. I make sure to keep the side I decorated face down.

"We agreed to keep whatever we discussed today confidential," Mom says. "So you don't have to worry about the other kids finding out before you're ready to tell them."

"Ready to tell them? Don't you get it, Mom? I'll never be ready to tell them. Besides, if that's true, why did you just tell me Camila didn't speak for two years after her father died? And that Antoine found his brother? Weren't those things supposed to be confidential too?"

Mom sighs. "Did anyone ever tell you'd make a good lawyer?"

"I'm going to be a paramedic. You know that."

We cross three intersections before Mom speaks again. "You good with frozen pizza for supper?" She is switching to a neutral subject. I hope that means she'll let me stay home tomorrow. She can go to grief retreat without me and *share*.

"Pizza's fine. But I'm not going back tomorrow," I say, testing her.

We're stopped at a red light, so Mom turns to look at me. Her face is blank. I can't tell if she is about to give me a lecture or tell me I can stay home. I flip the mask over, then back over again—I don't want Mom to see how I decorated it. "Suit yourself," she says.

At home, Mom takes the pizza out of the freezer and preheats the oven. I make the Caesar salad. I beat an egg yolk for the dressing, then add a spoonful of mustard, some oil and vinegar and a spoonful of garlic powder. Mom rubs the back of my arm as I grate in the Parmesan cheese. "Dad's recipe," she whispers.

"Aren't you going to say I'm just like him?" I ask her. She says it so often I expect it. Like a chorus in a song.

Mom releases my arm, but she is still standing so close I can hear her breathing. "Maybe I've been saying it too much...maybe I've been putting pressure on you by comparing you to your father all the time."

"Is that something they told you at grief retreat?"

I don't wait for Mom's answer. I march out of the kitchen, slamming the door behind me. I don't want frozen pizza or Caesar salad.

I don't care that it's too early to go to bed. I don't care that my stomach is rumbling.

I hear my mom rattling around in the kitchen. I don't care that she will have to eat supper alone. I'm sick of worrying about how she is doing without a husband. I'm sick of worrying about the pills she takes. I don't just need a break from grief retreat. I need a break from her.

A wave of tiredness hits me. I didn't do much today—the silent walk wasn't exactly exercise—but now I don't have the energy to play chess online or open a book. And because the TV's in the basement, watching TV isn't an option anymore.

I don't even bother taking off my shirt or pants or brushing my teeth before I get into bed.

I pull the top sheet up to my chin. Already I can feel my surroundings getting blurry the way they do when I am in between being awake and asleep. For the first time since Dad's death, my mind isn't asking *what if* questions.

My eyelids feel heavy. It feels good to be able to fall asleep easily for a change.

I'm back at the intersection where my mom and I were stopped before. The grief mask is on my lap.

When I turn my head, I see a city bus has pulled up next to us.

The driver salutes me. And then I see his eyes—one brown, one hazel. What's Dad doing driving a city bus?

Now I'm on the bus too. Only it doesn't have seats inside the way buses do. And the floor has red and black squares on it, like a chessboard. Someone has turned this bus into a gym. That's me doing a barbell squat. I catch my reflection in the bus window. Sweat is pouring off my face. My eyes are bloodshot.

The bus lurches forward, but when I look toward the front of the bus, there's a chess pawn sitting where the driver should be. My dad has come to spot me. When he hooks his arms under mine, I know I'll be able to lift the barbell.

Felicia is on the bus too. She's crouched on the floor across from us, recording video on her cell phone.

It's the sound of my dad's voice that wakes me up. He is saying, "It's too much weight for you, Son."

I lie in bed and replay my dad's words in my head over and over again. I've missed him, but until now I didn't realize how much I missed the sound of his voice. I'll never hear his voice again.

I hear shuffling outside my door, and I smell pizza.

I wait until I hear my mother's door click shut before I get out of bed and eat my dinner.

SEVENTEEN

Abby

So here I am at the barbecue-chicken joint, trapped between my dad and Gustavo. Camila and Raquel are sitting across from us.

We came in separate cars, and I can't help noticing that Raquel has put on lipstick. I consider that a bad sign. What I don't get is why any woman would be interested in my dad. Can't she tell he's a total doofus?

There is a laminated card on our table with a list of desserts. Camila is practicing her reading. "Key l-l-"

"Lime," I snap. "Key lime pie. It's green."

My dad gives me a sharp look. But Camila's feelings are not hurt. "Key lime pie," she says in a satisfied way. "I love the color green." Then she points to the next item on the list and shows me the picture of the cake next to it. "Bos-Boston cream pie." Camila grins. "That looks yummy."

Now Camila peeks out at me from behind the dessert list. "I'm glad you got over that tantrum you had in the school lobby," she whispers, but it's loud enough that everyone can hear, even the people in the next booth. "I have tantrums sometimes, and I always feel bad after. Do you feel bad now?"

"Not really." I know my dad is listening, but I'm back to ignoring him.

The thing is, I don't see why we had to come here.

Mom called barbecue chicken *comfort food*. Even before she got sick, when she'd had a long day at the school where she was vice-principal, Chalet Barbecue was our go-to place. Sometimes we'd get takeout, but mostly the three of us used to go there together. Mom liked that they hadn't changed the décor since she was a kid growing up in Montreal. *There's a certain comfort*, she used to say, *in things staying the same*. Same knotty-pine wood paneling on the walls, same Formica tabletops and vinyl seats that make squishy sounds when you slide into your spot.

Apparently the menu hasn't changed either. Same chicken with greasy skin, and soggy fries with barbecue sauce, hamburger bun and coleslaw on the side. Chicken salad and a chicken club are on the menu, but no one ever orders them. Even the waitress hasn't changed. It's still the same middle-aged woman with her hair in a messy bun and a pencil tucked behind one ear.

The waitress nodded when she saw my dad and me come in. But she didn't ask about my mom or offer condolences.

She must've figured out my mom died. She would have known she was sick, because we used to come in here with the VAD, and I remember Mom explaining to her about the suitcase.

At least Dad knew enough not to sit at *our* booth—the one in the front window, overlooking Sherbrooke Street and the Décarie Expressway.

"Will it be one bill?" the waitress asks when she comes over. I can see her checking out Raquel and the kids, wondering who they are and how we know them.

"That would be fine," my dad tells her.

"Separate bills," Raquel says over him. She points to Camila and Gustavo. "We're together."

That makes me relax a little. I guess Raquel doesn't want to give my dad the impression they're on a date.

Once we've ordered, Camila lays her hand flat on the middle of the table and gives her brother an expectant look.

"I'm too tired to play," Gustavo tells her. "And too hungry. The fries smell really good."

"C'mon, pretty please," Camila says.

Gustavo puts his hand on top of his sister's. Then she lays her hand on top of his and looks over at me. "Do you wanna play? It's more fun with more kids."

I start to say no, but then I figure it's not worth resisting. The food here never takes more than five minutes to get to the table. A half dozen rounds of hand stack, and I'll be gnawing on a drumstick.

In the background I hear Dad tell Raquel that he is a mechanical engineer, and then he is naming off all the bridges around Montreal that he helped build. Raquel is pretending to be interested, but I catch her swallowing a yawn—twice.

I can't remember the last time I heard Dad talk so much. When he runs out of bridges, he looks past me to Gustavo. "So I understand you're Eugene's assistant this weekend. That sounds like a big honor. How's it working out?"

Gustavo pulls his hand out of the stack so he can focus on the question.

Camila makes a pouty face.

"It's going all right, I guess," Gustavo tells my dad. "It's hard for kids the first year. I know because it was hard for me. I didn't want to talk about my feelings or my papi. I was hurting too much. All the other kids in our group are new this year. There's this guy, Antoine. His baby brother died of SIDS. But Antoine talks more about how his two moms are doing than how he feels. Then there's this guy, Christopher. He won't say what happened to his father."

I catch Dad and Raquel glancing at each other when Gustavo says this.

"D'you know what happened to Chris—" I start to ask Raquel (since I'm not speaking to my dad), but Gustavo talks over me. He keeps talking even when the waitress comes back with our chicken.

"Felicia is a bit wild. Maybe it's because both her parents are d—" Gustavo stops himself, and I decide it's because he doesn't want to upset Camila. "And, of course, there's Abby. She makes good jokes."

I tuck the edge of my napkin under my collar. This could get messy. "I thought you didn't like my jokes," I say to Gustavo. "I thought you said they were angry."

Gustavo reaches across the table so he can cut Camila's chicken into small pieces. "They *are* angry. But they're still funny."

Dad dips two fries into his barbecue sauce. He is a methodical eater. He always finishes all his fries before he starts on his chicken leg. "Abby's mother had a great sense of humor too."

I turn to look at him, but he doesn't notice because he is concentrating on his French fries. It's the first time in ages he's mentioned my mom.

"But her jokes were never angry," he adds.

What I wish I could ask him (if I was talking to him) is how he can sit here at *our* restaurant, wolfing down fries, and not miss my mom. Because right now I miss her so much I can't even take a bite of my drumstick.

At least Gustavo knows not to talk while he's eating, but between bites he tells Dad more about what it's like to be Eugene's assistant. "To be honest," Gustavo says, "I'm kinda worried about Eugene. I know he's in great shape, but he got really sweaty on our walk today."

"Gustavo is very good at worrying," Camila adds brightly.

"It did get pretty warm out today," I say to Gustavo. "I was sweating too."

Raquel reaches across the table and pats Gustavo's hand. "Camila is right. You know what worries me, *hijo*? How much *you* worry…"

"It's because of what happened to Papi," Camila says.

That Camila is pretty smart for a six-year-old.

Camila eyes my drumstick. "Are you going to eat that? Or can I have it?"

"Camila!" Raquel says. "Be polite."

"Are you going to eat that? Or *please* can I have it?" Camila asks.

I tell Camila she can have what's left of my drumstick. I pick at the French fries. Maybe my appetite is coming back.

It turns out not to be such a bad night out.

When we are leaving, I try not to look at the booth in the front window. But Dad nudges me when we go by. He doesn't say anything, but in this case he doesn't have to.

Because we are parked on opposite sides of the street, we say goodbye to Raquel and the kids outside Chalet Barbecue.

We are about to get into our car when I hear Camila calling from across the street. "So are you and my mami boyfriend and girlfriend now?" she asks.

I could get upset.

Dad could get embarrassed.

Instead, Dad and I do something we hardly ever do— we laugh at the same time.

EIGHTEEN

Christopher

Because I'm in the kitchen before Mom, I measure out the coffee and put her espresso pot on the stove—the way Dad always did.

"You didn't have to do that," she says when she walks into the kitchen. She doesn't mention Dad.

If she is surprised to see me downstairs, she doesn't say so.

"What time do we need to leave?" I ask.

"I thought you weren't coming."

I nearly tell her about my dream, but something holds me back. For now, I want to keep it to myself. "I changed my mind," I tell her.

At the last second I remember that Eugene asked us to bring a photograph of the person we are grieving. There's a photo of Dad on our refrigerator. It's from the card we gave out at the funeral home. It says *Rest in peace* and it has Dad's date of birth and date of death on it. In the photo, Dad is wearing his red baseball cap with the words *Elite Squad* on it. He is grinning into the camera. The photo must have been taken before he started hiding out in his man cave.

"Is it okay with you if I bring this to grief retreat?" I ask Mom.

"Of course. I have a whole package of those cards left from the funeral."

I don't ask Mom what she is saving the cards for. She has used two magnets to stick the card on the fridge. I push them aside when I take down the card. One magnet has a banana on it, and the other has a woodpecker. I don't know why I never noticed that magnet before. "When did you get that magnet?" I ask, pointing at the woodpecker's red head.

"I've had that thing forever," she says. "Your dad gave it to me."

～

It's even warmer than yesterday, and Eugene and Gustavo have opened all the windows in the classroom.

"Did you manage to find a photograph of your folks?" Eugene asks Felicia when she comes in. She has on a different outfit today—but it's still all black.

Felicia takes one of those old-fashioned photo albums with the quilted covers out of her backpack. "I found this," she says, "at my grandparents' house. It's from my parents' wedding," she says softly.

She opens the album to a photograph of a couple standing in front of a picket fence with pink roses climbing up it.

"Wow, do you ever look like your dad," Abby says. It's true that Felicia has her dad's fair skin and pale blue eyes. If she didn't bleach her hair, maybe hers would be as dark as his.

Felicia snorts. "I wish I *didn't* look like him."

"Why not?" Abby asks. "Didn't you two get along?"

"We don't. I mean, we didn't." Felicia crosses her arms over her chest. "He found a girlfriend on the side."

"He *did*?" Abby sounds shocked.

Even I start to feel slightly sorry for Felicia. That must have sucked.

Eugene has a thermos of iced tea with him today. He opens the thermos and pours himself a cup. For a moment, the lemony scent of the tea fills the air. "You're probably not just mourning your parents' deaths," Eugene says to Felicia, "but also the fact that they had marriage trouble. That's hard on a kid. I'm sorry you had to go through that."

Felicia closes the album and pushes it away from her. Abby passes her the box of Kleenex, but Felicia doesn't take one.

"Okay," Eugene says, "how about we look at the rest of your pictures? Abby, what'd you bring us?"

Abby has brought a newspaper clipping. It's a story about her mother being named vice-principal of the year. Because the clipping looks like it has been folded and unfolded many times, the deep creases in the paper make it hard to see Abby's mother's face. "Being named vice-principal of the year is a big deal," Abby says. "There was a reception, and the director of the school board made a speech about my mom. Her whole career, she worked at inner-city schools where a lot of the kids were at risk of dropping out. The director talked about what a difference she made in kids' lives. They even invited some of the kids she'd worked with when she was a young teacher. Some of them"—Abby reaches for the Kleenex box—"came to the funeral."

Abby blows her nose. "Allergies," she says when she sees me looking at her. "I nearly brought a photo of her from the end. When she was stuck in bed all day. But I'm glad I decided to bring this instead."

Eugene nods as if Abby has said something very deep. "It sounds like you're pretty proud of your mom," he says.

"I was pr—"Abby corrects herself. "I *am* proud of her." Now she lowers her voice as if she is about to let us in on a secret. "But I remember that sometimes, when she'd come home late from school and all she wanted to talk about was this student or that student, well…sometimes I thought she cared more about them than she cared about me."

Felicia shakes her head. "I can't believe you said that, Abby! Of course she cared more about *you*. You were her daughter."

Eugene raises his palm in the air. Abby blows her nose again. "What matters," he says, "is how Abby felt and how she feels now. Every feeling is real and deserves to be acknowledged."

"Antoine." Eugene's voice softens. "Were you able to find a picture of Vincent?"

Antoine takes out a brown envelope he's been keeping on his lap. Inside is one of those department-store family photographs—I can tell from the navy-blue curtains in the background. Antoine is holding a baby. Vincent has spiky black hair and round dark eyes.

"What's with the hai—" Felicia catches herself before she can say something mean.

I nearly point out that she's got spiky hair herself.

"Is that your mom?" Abby asks, pointing at a smiling woman in the photograph.

"Uh-huh," Antoine says. "That was when we were a family."

"You're still a family," Eugene says gently.

I have been folding over the edges of the card with the picture of my dad on it. I can feel my brain working overtime. What Eugene just said about Antoine and his moms still being a family applies to me and my mom too. And what Abby said before about feeling like her mom cared more about her students than about her—it's like her words poked something in me that's been balled up in a corner of my heart. Maybe I felt that way about my dad too. That he cared more about the people he helped than about me and my mom. I nearly say so, only Gustavo jumps in to tell us about the photo he has brought with him.

He has been keeping the photo face down, but now he flips it over as if we're in for a giant surprise. Like we are playing cards and he's about to pull out an ace.

When I look at the photo, I am surprised. That's because it's a black-and-white shot of a small boy wearing a striped T-shirt. There are snowcapped mountains in the background. "That's my papi," Gustavo tells us, "in Chile."

"How old do you think he is in that picture?" Eugene asks.

"Mami says he was probably four or five. So even younger than Camila is now."

Abby leans in to inspect the photo. "He looks happy," she says.

Felicia studies the photo too. "Look at those mountains. Do you happen to know where in Chile the photo was taken?"

Gustavo shrugs. "I could ask Mami."

"How does the photo make you feel?" Eugene asks.

"Sad," Gustavo says. Then he does something I haven't seen him do before. He stops to think before he speaks. "Sad but also good."

Abby turns to me. "Guess who's last for show-and-tell?" she says.

I pass around the picture of my dad. I see Antoine looking at the dates underneath the photograph, calculating how old my dad was when he died. "Forty-two," I tell him.

I take a deep breath.

"My dad was forty-two when he killed himself."

NINETEEN

Abby

Christopher's dad committed suicide.

It's the very worst thing I've ever heard at grief retreat. Even worse than Felicia watching her parents drown or Antoine finding his baby brother dead. No wonder Christopher didn't want us to know.

So far at grief retreat, every time someone says something, somebody else—usually Eugene or Gustavo—makes a comment. But when Christopher says, *My dad was forty-two when he killed himself* no one says a word. Not Eugene, not Gustavo. I don't even hear the sound of traffic outside on Sherbrooke Street. It's as if the whole world comes to a stop.

I don't look at Felicia, because I know if our eyes meet she will find a way to send me a message saying *I told you so*. Felicia was right. Christopher's father did not die saving someone else's life. He was not a hero.

I bet the others are wondering the same thing as me—how did Christopher's father do it? But even if we all want to know, none of us dares to ask. Not even Felicia, who's the nosiest person on Planet Grief and also, quite possibly, on Planet Earth.

Gustavo passes me the photo Christopher brought with him today. The first thing I notice is how alike Christopher and his dad look. It's not just the different-colored eyes, but also the way they hold their heads at an angle. The next thing I notice is how healthy Christopher's father looks. His cheeks are full, not sunken like my mom's were before she died. His skin is tanned, and his eyes look bright and hopeful, as if he is in on some joke he can't tell us.

How, I wonder, could a perfectly healthy person take his own life when my mom would have given anything to have a heart that worked? It doesn't make sense.

Now that Christopher has started telling his story, he can't stop. Are we the first people he has told about his father's death? Maybe it's because he's been telling the story inside his head for so long that it comes out so easily.

Christopher starts his story at the end.

"I found him," he says. "In the basement. Every morning, when he'd come in from an overnight shift, he'd go straight to the basement. Sometimes we'd hear him watching TV. Other times, he'd just sit there in the dark. I used to ask Mom if I could go in and talk to him, but she told me it was better to let him be—that with a job like his, he needed some alone time.

"The day he...he...did it...the TV was on for longer than usual. And he didn't come up to the kitchen to grab some cereal or a coffee the way he sometimes did. My mom was making espresso, and I told her I'd bring him a cup. "Just make sure he's not asleep when you go in," she told me.

"So that's what I thought when I found him. That he was asleep. And I remember being happy for him—because I knew he often had trouble falling asleep after an overnight shift. He was in his recliner, with his feet propped up. But his head was slumped over in a way I'd never seen before. Kind of like a ragdoll without its stuffing. At first I thought I'd let him rest, but there was something about the angle of his head that didn't look right. And he wasn't snoring. We were always teasing him about how loud he snored.

"Dad!" I said—I remember I didn't shout because I didn't want Mom to think something was wrong. "Dad!" I said again. "You all right? I brought you coffee. No milk, no sugar. Just the way you like it."

"By then I was close enough that I should've heard him breathing. But he wasn't breathing. And when I reached out to touch him, his hand was cold and clammy. That's when I tried to yell for my mom. Only no sound came out."

Christopher has lowered his head, and I can't help wondering if that's the position his dad was in when Christopher found him.

Now a sound comes out of Christopher that I've never heard before. It's not a sob or a wail or a moan. It's a dry sound, and I think, That's what pain sounds like.

Felicia kicks me hard under the table. I shake my head no. I still won't look at her. I know what she's thinking—that she wishes she could record all this for her dumb documentary. Doesn't she have feelings? Can't she see how terrible Christopher feels?

"He overdosed on painkillers," Christopher says, answering the question we're all wondering about. "I found two empty pill bottles on the carpet by his chair. He'd been taking meds for his shoulder. Mom said he must have been stockpiling pills. When I got my voice back, I yelled at my mom to call 9-1-1. The paramedics who responded to the call—they were Dad's colleagues."

"How could he do that to you?" Almost right away, I regret blurting out the question.

Christopher doesn't look at me when he answers. "I ask myself that all the time," he says. "We should've known my dad had PTSD. The people he worked with should have figured it out too. The man cave stuff—he never used to do that. He used to hang out with us when he got home from work. We should've recognized the signs." Christopher shakes his head.

I wince as I picture the scene. Christopher's dad slumped over in his easy chair. Christopher trying to shout but not having a voice. The paramedics showing up at the door.

And then I realize something else. Christopher never got a chance to say goodbye to his dad.

At least I got to say goodbye to my mom.

Christopher swallows before he starts speaking again. "I don't know if I can forgive him for what he did."

Eugene squeezes Christopher's elbow and makes a point of looking him in the eye. "One day, Christopher, you might be able to forgive him. I really hope that'll happen. But there's someone else you're gonna need to forgive. And that could be even harder."

I think I know who Eugene is talking about.

Christopher needs to forgive himself.

"I found my brother," Antoine says now.

Felicia turns to look at Antoine. "Didn't you say your moms found him? That they screamed so loud they woke up the downstairs neighbors?"

Antoine shakes his head. "They did scream. But I'm the one who found him. And there's something else I didn't tell you." Antoine pauses. "I should have checked to make sure the monitor was charged. But..." Antoine starts to choke up.

I pat his back. "It's okay," I tell him, mostly because I don't know what else to say.

"I should've recharged it," Antoine says. "I was playing *Battlefield 1* with a kid from school. If the battery was charged, we might have heard something, and Vincent might not have died."

Eugene exhales slowly. "You don't know that," he tells Antoine. "But that's a big burden to carry around. It's good you told us."

Antoine nods. Christopher hands him a Kleenex, and Antoine blows his nose.

I'm tearing up a little myself. No one warned me grief retreat could break my heart.

"Eugene. Are you there?" A woman's voice is coming through the intercom by the classroom door. I think it's Raquel.

Eugene sprints over to the intercom.

"This is Eugene," he says. "Raquel, is that you? Is everything okay downstairs?"

Raquel's voice comes crackling through the intercom. "There's something strange going on. Someone just phoned the school. She says her name is Felicia. Felicia Symatowksi."

TWENTY

Christopher

Checkmate!

I was right!

Felicia is not Felicia Symatowski.

She is some twisted grief-retreat stalker. And I just told her the story of my dad's suicide! If she were a guy I'd punch her. "I knew you were up to something! This is... this is disgusting!" I am so angry, I have trouble getting my words out.

Abby shouts, "If you're not Felicia Symatowksi, who are you? And why are you pretending to be someone else? What you've done is really wrong! I trusted you, Felicia—or whatever your name is!"

"I'm very upset," Eugene is saying. "And I don't know how this could have happened. Who are you, and what are you doing at our grief retreat?"

"Yeah," Antoine says, "who are you?"

I move in so close to Fake Felicia that we are just inches apart. "Your name is Jessie Towers, isn't it?" And now I think the others must also be remembering how, during the silent walk yesterday, someone mistook her for Jessie Towers. Only I'm sure now that it wasn't a mistake!

If Felicia—I need to stop calling her that—was a decent person, she'd apologize, but she doesn't. "I can explain everything," she says instead. "This is all just a slight misunderstanding."

"A *slight misunderstanding*?" I shout so loudly that the classroom windows rattle. "You lied to us about who you are. We told you all kinds of private stuff about our lives. That's way bigger than *a slight misunderstanding!*" And now something else occurs to me. "I bet that whole story you told us about your parents drowning on the lake is one giant lie, isn't it?"

Abby puts her hand over her mouth. I wonder how she feels about her BFF now.

Fake Felicia hangs her head. "Okay, I admit it. I made that part up," she says. She still hasn't apologized. "I didn't mean any harm."

Abby's mouth drops open. "You didn't mean any harm? Don't you see what you've done? You lied to us. I believed that story about your parents. I felt so bad for you. I thought you were so courageous. But you were just messing with us. How could you do that? I bet you don't even like blue-cheese dressing."

Blue-cheese dressing? What's that got to do with anything?

Gustavo shakes his head. "This has never happened at grief retreat before. It's a big, big problem."

Eugene wrings his hands. "This was supposed to be a safe space," he says. "And you've violated that safe space, Felicia—or Jessie, or whatever your name is. What you've done is beyond wrong. It's cruel."

Fake Felicia bites her lip. "Okay, okay, I see your point, and I'm sorry."

It sure took her long enough to apologize.

"But if you'll just let me ex—" Her voice breaks.

"All right," Eugene says, "go ahead and explain. But this time, you've got to tell us the truth. And when you're done, I'm going to let the other kids decide how they want to handle this situation."

"Christopher's right," Fake Felicia says, and I can't hold back a smug smile. Who doesn't love being right? "My name *is* Jessie Towers. But I swear I wasn't planning any of this. A few weeks ago I saw a poster outside the guidance counselor's office at my school, advertising the grief retreat. I thought it would make an amazing documentary fil—"

I jump in. "I caught her in the bathroom yesterday. She'd been videotaping our session."

"What were you doing in the girls' bathroom?" Abby asks me. From her tone, you'd think I was the one who did something wrong, not Jessie.

"She was in the boys' bathroom. This is an all-boys school," I remind Abby.

Eugene's eyes look like they're about to jump out of their sockets. He puts his hands on his hips. "Is it true that you taped yesterday's session?" he asks Felicia. "Because that would be totally unethical."

"I didn't do it on purpose."

When Jessie looks down at the floor, I know she is lying. She did do it on purpose. I'm sure she was shooting video for her documentary.

"I made her delete it," I tell the others.

Jessie looks down at the floor again. Then she looks back up at us and raises her palms in the air. "If you could just let me finish. Please."

Gustavo is being unusually quiet. But now he says, "Let's let her finish."

"I just thought I'd drop by at the beginning of the grief retreat and tell you guys about my idea for the documentary film. I really thought—and I still think—that a film about how kids grieve would be amazing. A lot of kids don't have resources like this." She gestures around the classroom, then at Eugene. "Or someone like you, who knows how to help them."

Eugene doesn't smile. Jessie is trying to butter him up, and I'm glad he's not falling for it.

"And then, well, one thing led to another, and then, well, I saw Felicia Symatowski's name on the list, and Gustavo said he was sorry that both my parents had died. And then, well, I came up with the story." Jessie's voice gets higher when says *came up with the story*—as if she's impressed by her own imagination. Who cares if she hurt a bunch of people along the way? "Like I said, I'm really, really, really, super sorry. I get a little carried away sometimes."

"Carried away?" I say. "*Carried away* makes it sound like you had nothing to do with it. Like you're not responsible for your actions. Like you're not evil." *Evil* is a strong word, but it feels right.

Eugene has been watching Jessie's face. He is scrunching up his forehead, trying to figure something out. "There's one thing I want to know...Jessie. What got you so interested in grief in the first place?"

Jessie closes her eyes and inhales deeply. Without meaning to, I inhale deeply too. Is it possible that this girl who has been trying since yesterday morning to steal our secrets has her own secret? Or is she about to tell us another lie?

"Did someone you love die?" Gustavo whispers. "Is that why you came to grief retreat?"

"How do we know we can trust what's she going to tell us?" Abby asks. "I'll never be able to trust her."

Good point.

Jessie sighs. "I swear that everything I tell you from now on will be 100 percent true."

Abby crosses her arms over her chest. She still won't look Jessie in the eye.

"No one died," Jessie says. "But my dad took off six months ago. My mom says she didn't even realize there was something wrong. It turns out he'd had a girlfriend for over a year. Someone he knew from high school. She friended him on Facebook. How cheesy is that?" Jessie looks up at all of us. "The part about living with my grandparents is true. My mom and I couldn't afford to stay in the house, so we had to move in with them. It's pretty cramped, all of us in one tiny apartment."

"There are worse things in the world than being stuck in a tiny apartment," I mutter. "Being a liar is one of them."

For the first time since we found out Jessie is an imposter, Abby looks her in the eye. "D'you still see your father?"

"Nope, not anymore. At first, he phoned and texted. I told him I was too upset to see him. Then he stopped trying to contact me."

Gustavo raises his hand. "Your father might have run off with his girlfriend. But I'd like to point one thing out. You still *have* a father."

TWENTY-ONE

Abby

I can't believe how easily I let Felicia—Jessie—fool me.

I felt so bad for her when she told that story about seeing her parents die out on the frozen lake. But that's all it was—a story.

I'm so angry at Jessie for lying, I could burst.

I'm also angry at myself for believing her! How could I have been so gullible? Maybe it's because I was desperate for a best friend who had gone through the same thing as me. But Jessie isn't that friend. Gustavo's right. Jessie still *has* a father. So what if she doesn't get to see him? That can always change, and it probably will. The rest of us will never get another second with the loved one we are grieving.

Eugene mops his forehead with a hankie. "As I said, I'm going to leave it to you kids to decide how we handle this situation. Jessie, I want you to wait outside the classroom while the kids discuss what's happened and how they want to proceed."

Jessie gets up from her spot at the table. "I'm sorry," she whispers when she passes behind me, "for impersonating Felicia Symatowski. I shouldn't have done it. And for the record, blue-cheese dressing really is my favorite." Then she looks at the other kids. "I'll be outside."

She goes out into the hallway just outside the classroom.

I get up to close the door. I make a point of looking over Jessie's head. I want her to know I cannot forgive her.

Eugene interlaces his fingers on the table and cracks his knuckles. "First off," he says, "I want to apologize. What happened today should never have happened. This is *your* grief retreat. Like I said, I'm going to leave it up to you folks to decide how to handle this. Let's start with a bit of discussion about how you're feeling right now."

I surprise myself by being the first to speak. "I don't know if I'll ever be able to forgive her. Also, I feel like a total idiot for believing Jessie's stories in the first place." It feels weird to call her Jessie.

"We all believed her," Antoine says.

"I didn't," Christopher says. "But I should've reported the cell-phone business sooner. I didn't want to be a rat."

"I don't know about the rest of you," Gustavo says, "but I feel a bit sorry for her. I know what she did was wrong, but it must be sad having a father and not seeing him."

"It's not the same thing at all," I remind him. "You said so yourself. Besides, this is a grief retreat for kids mourning the *death* of someone they love."

"What about that documentary she wants to make?" Antoine asks.

Christopher makes a snorting sound. "I can't believe you're thinking about the documentary. What Jessie did is practically a crime. It's called identity theft."

Gustavo raises his hand. "Identity theft is when someone steals your credit card. We're too young for credit cards."

I'm still thinking about what an idiot I was for believing Jessie's stories. "I vote we kick her out. She's a liar. She doesn't belong here with us."

Eugene waits to see if anyone has anything else to add. "All right then," he says, when he's satisfied there's no more discussion. "Let's take it to a vote. Lay your heads down on the table. That way you won't be influenced by how someone else is voting."

We put our heads down.

"Who votes to let Jessie stay for the rest of this grief retreat?"

I keep both of my hands flat on the table.

I hear stirring across from me. Without moving my forehead, I lift one cheek. I see a pair of hands flat on the table across from me.

"Moving right along." Eugene's voice doesn't give anything away. "How many of you vote to ask Jessie to leave?"

"I do," I say, but then I cover my mouth. I raise my hand. I can hear the sounds of other kids raising their hands too. Will it be unanimous?

"One, two…" Eugene gets to three. "You can sit up now," he tells us. "We have our decision. Three of you voted for Jessie to leave. One person voted to let her stay. The majority rules. Let's call Jessie back in to let her know your decision."

Jessie hangs her head while Eugene breaks the news. He doesn't mention that someone voted for her to stay. "Before you leave the building," Eugene tells her, "I want you to promise that you will keep everything you learned at grief retreat confidential. Can you make that promise?"

"I can," Jessie says.

"Anyone can make a promise," Christopher says. "The question is, can you keep the promise?"

Jessie swallows. "I can."

"I'm glad we have your word," Eugene tells her. "I also want to let you know that there are support groups for kids whose parents have split up. If you leave me your email, I'd be glad to get you the names of some counselors who run that kind of group. That sort of support might do you a lot of good."

"Maybe she could make a documentary about a support group for kids whose parents are divorced," Christopher mutters.

"Thanks for the tip," Jessie tells him. "Much appreciated." She stuffs her sweater into her backpack and picks up her half-finished grief mask from the table. I wonder how she was planning to decorate her *inside* mask.

We all watch as she grabs her phone from the pile on the table. I figure she'll skulk out of the room, but she doesn't. Not right away anyhow. Instead, she turns the phone over and scans the screen for messages before putting it in her back pocket. That's when I know for sure she isn't really sorry about what she did to us. "I'm glad I got to meet all of you," she says quietly. She sounds like she means it.

But I don't fall for it. I bet that sounding sorry is just another one of Jessie's acts.

I don't watch her go. None of us say a word—not until she's had time to leave the school.

Christopher catches Eugene's eye. "I'd like permission to use my cell phone, please."

"What for?" Eugene asks him. "I thought you were in favor of making this a cell-phone-free zone."

"It's for research purposes," Christopher says. "I think we should check out Jessie Towers's Instagram posts."

I suddenly realize what Christopher is thinking. The girl who recognized Jessie on the street yesterday mentioned an Instagram account. What had she said about Jessie's comments? That they were *wicked*. I take a deep breath. "I'd like to see it too," I say.

"The account could be private," Antoine points out.

"All right," Eugene says, "I can understand why you'd be curious. Heck, I'm curious myself." He hands us back our phones—and takes his own phone out of his pocket. "Do I just google Instagram?" he asks.

"You need to be on Instagram," Antoine explains. "Let me do it. Here she is—Jessie Towers, Montreal. The account isn't private." Antoine whistles. "She's got over a thousand followers."

I am looking at Jessie's Instagram page on my phone too. There's a photo of her with her mom, whom I recognize from the wedding photos Jessie showed us. And another photo of Jessie and a friend sticking out their tongues and laughing into the camera. For a second I feel jealous. I wanted her to be *my* friend. Until I found out she was a fake.

I scroll down to a photo Jessie has tagged and commented on. In it, an overweight girl is wearing a neon-orange bikini. All the comments are gushing (**Love your bikini**, **You look A-mazing**, **Orange is so your color**), except for Jessie's. She has written, **Happy Halloween, you glow-in-the-dark PUMPKIN**. The comment and the way she capitalized the word *pumpkin* makes me wince.

"Her Facebook page is public too," Christopher calls out. "But there isn't much here. Links to some documentary film festival. Hmm," he says. "This gets a little more interesting."

"What'd you find?" Gustavo asks.

"A link to an article in *Psychology Today*. '*Tips for getting people to open up to you*,'" Christopher says.

Gustavo tries to read over Christopher's shoulder. "What are the tips?" he asks.

Christopher is so focused on the article, he doesn't hear Gustavo's question.

Gustavo nudges Christopher. "So what does it say?"

"*Tip number one*," Christopher reads out loud from the article, "*is to build sympathy with the person. A good way to do this is by sharing a difficult life experience.*"

"That's what Eugene did when he told us how he lived on the streets," Gustavo says.

"And it's what Jessie tried to do when she told us that story about watching her parents drown," I add.

"*Tip number two*," Christopher continues. "*Emphasize traits you have in common with the person.*"

Blue-cheese dressing, I think to myself. "She was using us," I tell the others. "I'm so angry I could spit."

Christopher turns off his phone and slides it back to the middle of the table. I guess he's had enough of the article. "Me too," he says.

Antoine shakes the hair out of his eyes. "I'm glad we made her leave."

Gustavo stays quiet, confirming my hunch that he was the one who voted to let Jessie stay.

Eugene sighs. "I think we're all feeling like Jessie betrayed us—and manipulated us. That feeling makes us angry, not just with Jessie, but with ourselves too—for falling into her trap."

I think I'm angrier with myself for believing Jessie's stories than I am with Jessie for making them up.

"There's nothing wrong with feeling angry," Eugene says. "All weekend we've been discussing how important it is to tune into our feelings. But it's also possible that your anger—*our* anger," Eugene corrects himself, "isn't only about Jessie. Maybe Jessie's given us a focal point for all the anger we've got stored up inside and haven't had been able to express."

I look up at Eugene. "You make it sound like that's a good thing. Like we should feel grateful to her for lying."

Eugene chuckles—even though I wasn't joking. "You might be on to something, Abby. In any case, kids, I think we should try moving on to another exercise. But if you want or need to talk more about Jessie, we can always come back to it."

I want to forget all about Jessie. "What's the new exercise?" I ask.

The exercise sounds lame. Instead of us telling our *own* stories, Eugene wants us to tell the story of the person sitting next to us. He says it's for empathy building. "It's a way to take you out of the story of your own life and into somebody else's," he explains.

So much for forgetting about Jessie. Because when Eugene mentions getting into another person's life, I think about her and how she invented a story for herself and her parents. Do all liars have overactive imaginations?

"Why don't you start, Christopher?" Eugene says.

Because we are sitting next to each other, Christopher tells my story. "Abby's mom died in March. She caught a virus that weakened her heart. She was on the list for a heart transplant, but she didn't get it in time." Christopher sighs when he says that. There is a weird comfort in hearing somebody else tell my story—and feel upset for me that my mom did not stay alive long enough to get a new heart.

"Did I get that right?" Christopher asks when he's done.

"Yup," I tell him. "Thanks." I close my eyes for a second, and when I do, I think about the part of the story the others don't know. How I had the virus before my mom. I push the thought away.

When Gustavo starts telling Christopher's story, he surprises me by keeping it short, maybe because it's so hard to tell. "Christopher's dad was a paramedic. He saved a lot of people, but when he got PTSD—that stands for post-traumatic stress disorder—he didn't know how to ask for help for himself." Gustavo pauses, then swallows twice. "He committed suicide by overdosing on pills. Christopher found him."

"Antoine found his brother," I say as I begin telling Antoine's story. "Vincent was only three months old. He died of SIDS, which stands for sudden infant death syndrome." I don't mention the baby monitor. "Antoine has a *maman* and a mom. His mom's been depr—" I correct myself. "She's been dealing with the deep sadness of grief."

Antoine tells Gustavo's story. "This is Gustavo's third year at grief retreat. His father died of lung cancer, even though he never smoked. Gustavo has a little sister named Camila." Antoine catches Gustavo's eye. "Did I leave anything out?"

"You could say I'm Eugene's assistant," Gustavo says.

"He doesn't have to. You just said it," I point out.

"What about your story, Eugene? Who's going to tell it?" Antoine asks.

We look around the table. We've all had a turn. "Why don't we tell it together?" I suggest.

"Good idea," Eugene says, leaning back in his chair to listen.

Christopher starts. "Eugene's mom had cancer too. She was sick for a while."

Antoine picks up the story. "Eugene was the youngest in his family, and the others thought he was too little to understand what was going on. So they never explained anything to him. He never had a chance to say goodbye or to grieve."

"He went through some hard times afterward," I say.

I'm about to get into the hard times when Gustavo interrupts. "He lived on the streets."

I continue with the story. After all, I hardly got to say anything before Gustavo cut me off. "Once Eugene was able to do his grieving, things started to get better for him. He even met his wife at the grief support group he went to. They have twins."

Gustavo raises his hand. "Two of them."

I roll my eyes. "That's pretty much the definition of twins. They come in twos."

TWENTY-TWO

Christopher

We're working on our inside masks. Eugene hands me a new pile of magazines.

I am about to start flipping through the first one when I look out the window. There's Jessie sitting in the bus-stop shelter. A bus stops, blocking my view. When the bus drives off, I look back at the shelter, expecting the bench where Jessie was sitting to be empty. But she hasn't moved.

Instead of looking through the magazine, I grab a sheet of paper from the cabinet and write out a document for Jessie to sign. Because I don't trust Jessie Towers to keep her promise.

I, Jessie Towers, hereby state that I will not use any personal information that was disclosed during the grief retreat that took place in Montreal on May 5-6, 2018.

Signed in Montreal on this 6th day of May 2018.

_____ *(Signature)*

_____ *(Witness)*

Antoine looks over my shoulder. "What is that?"

"Insurance," I tell him.

Abby reads the document out loud. "It sounds like a lawyer wrote it," she says. "But how are you going to deliver it to Jessie? She left."

I point out the window. "No, she didn't."

The other kids get up to see.

"She's waiting for the bus," Gustavo says.

"No, she isn't. The bus just passed, and she didn't take it."

When I get downstairs, Jessie is still sitting in the shelter. She waves when she sees me. Does she honestly think I've come to invite her back into the grief retreat? I hand her the document and a pen. "If you could sign this. Please."

I don't say a word as she reads and signs the document. She gives me back the pen and paper, and I sign where it says *Witness*. Then, without saying goodbye, I turn around and head back into the school.

Maybe now I can think about my inside mask.

When I pick up the magazine again, I don't know what I'm looking for, only that I don't want to use cut-out letters like I did for the outside mask.

My outside mask is strong. The me I show to people is calm and logical. Maybe some of that comes from playing chess.

But what does my inside mask look like? Put another way, *Who am I when I'm not wearing my outside mask?*

I'm not sure I know the answer. Have I gotten so used to wearing my outside mask that I've forgotten who I am underneath it?

I flip through a women's magazine. There are photos of models wearing capes and coats with fur collars. At the back there's a recipe section with photos of colorful salads and pasta dishes with vegetables I've never seen before. I am about to toss the magazine when I see an ad for vitamins. What stops me is the image of a pill bottle with round white pills next to it. I cut out the pills.

I glue the picture of the pills onto the inside of my mask. Then I take a red marker and use it to color the rest of my inside mask. Red is the color of blood. There was no blood when I walked into the basement and found my dad. That would have made things even harder. But the red background and the pill bottle somehow feel right for my inside mask.

On the outside I have to be strong.

On the inside I am sick with grief.

Yesterday I was curious to look at what the other kids were doing with their grief masks. Not today. Today I'm too busy thinking about my own two masks. Will I ever be able to go around without my outside mask?

The sound of scissors snipping paper and the smell of white glue and felt pens reminds me of elementary school. For the first time since I arrived at grief retreat, I'm glad to be here.

It was hard to tell the others about my dad's suicide, but now I'm relieved I did. Eugene was right. Keeping my dad's suicide a secret was a burden.

I look at the outside of my grief mask. I study the words I collaged together and the photo of the barbell. Now I remember what my dad told me in my dream. That I was lifting too much weight.

I feel a hard lump in my throat.

I miss my dad so much.

I think I will always miss him.

I feel tears coming. I don't want the others to see me cry. Because I don't know where else to look, I study the sheet of newspaper Eugene and Gustavo have laid out on the table. They've layered four or five sheets. Maybe Eugene is worried grief retreat will have to pay a fine if we damage school property.

My elbow grazes the top layer of newspaper, and now the sheet of newspaper underneath is exposed. Someone's been hoarding newspapers at this school, because these ones date back to last July. There's no missing a headline in a giant bold font. *FOUR DEAD IN TRAGIC PILEUP ON HIGHWAY 20*. And underneath the headline, in bold smaller letters, *ONE WOMAN REMAINS IN CRITICAL CONDITION*.

I start reading.

It must have been a really gruesome accident. I know because the story says the Jaws of Life were needed to extract the sole survivor, a woman named Dolores Ridley, from one of the cars. The Jaws of Life are a hydraulic rescue device used when there is no other way to free an accident victim from a vehicle. Mrs. Ridley's husband and two other passengers died on impact. So did the driver of the truck they collided with.

When I finish reading the story, I look through the pile of papers for a follow-up article. I want to know if Dolores Ridley pulled through. The next two newspapers in my pile are from June 2017.

But now I find one from the third week of July. Tucked at the bottom of page four, I spot a small item. The headline reads **CRASH SURVIVOR IN STABLE CONDITION**.

This time there's a comment from the trauma doctor who handled her case. *Dolores Ridley's condition has stabilized. We were able to transfer her out of the intensive care unit. Though we expect Mrs. Ridley will remain in hospital for several more weeks, we are confident she is out of danger.*

"Amazing," I say out loud.

Antoine is trying on his mask. He gazes at me from behind the drawings he's made of his favorite video games. "What's amazing?"

I point to the newspaper in front of me. "Do you know about the Jaws of Life?"

TWENTY-THREE

Abby

I covered my outside mask with exclamation marks. I used felt pen, but when I saw how Christopher was cutting letters out of magazines, I got inspired to try that too. The only problem is that serious magazines like *Time* and *Maclean's* don't use a lot of exclamation marks. Now if there were some *National Enquirers* in Eugene's pile, I'd have had an easier time of it. *Human Mother Gives Birth to Baby Elephant!!! Elvis Presley Returns From the Dead for One Last Blowout Concert!!!*

The exclamation marks could be my way of saying I use humor for my outside mask. Maybe Gustavo was right about me. But hey, making sarcastic comments is better than fighting. When I'm upset and I crack a joke, I feel safer, more protected. It's like adding a layer of insulation when they build a house. I am a well-insulated girl.

But what's underneath my insulation?

Even asking myself the question in my head upsets me. Which makes me feel like coming up with a sarcastic joke. But instead I do what Eugene suggested (not that I'd ever admit to Eugene that I was following some of his advice).

Then the answer comes to me. Underneath my outside mask is fear. If I had to picture it, the fear would be cold and white. So I draw snowflakes inside my mask and add a snowman with a face like mine. It's a lot easier to make jokes than admit I am afraid. Afraid that what happened to my mom could happen to my dad—or even to me. Afraid of something I have never admitted to anyone else—that I gave my mom the virus that weakened her heart. So I draw a heart with an arrow through it, and I give my "snowgirl" a bow and arrow. I already know I'll never share my inside mask with the other kids.

I've been so busy drawing that I nearly miss an interesting conversation. Christopher has found a newspaper story about paramedics using something called the Jaws of Life to extract a woman from a car after a terrible accident.

"Paramedics only use the Jaws of Life in the worst cases," Christopher is explaining.

Maybe it's because of the name Jaws of Life that everyone wants to know more. Even Eugene.

Gustavo reaches for the first article and starts reading it. *"The sole survivor of the accident, Dolores Ridley, 43, was trapped in the car that her husband, Carl, was driving. Carl Ridley, 45, as well as the two other passengers in the car, Réal Thibodeau, 46, and Denise Champlain, 47, were killed on impact.*

Umberto Supino, 57, the driver of the truck involved in the accident, also died in the collision.

"Paramedics were able to use a device known as the Jaws of Life to extract Dolores Ridley from the car. According to Roger David, spokesperson for the Corporation of Quebec Paramedics, Ridley would almost certainly have died in the car had paramedics not intervened. Ridley was transferred to the McGill University Health Centre, where she remains in critical condition."

The second article quotes a trauma doctor who explains that Mrs. Ridley was transferred out of intensive care and is expected to survive.

I try to imagine what it must have been like for Mrs. Ridley to be the sole survivor of the accident—to wake up and learn that her husband was dead. The article doesn't say if the Ridleys had children.

The others are still talking about the Jaws of Life.

Gustavo looks at Christopher. "Do you think your dad could have been one of the paramedics who got Mrs. Ridley out of the car?"

Christopher shakes his head. "My dad committed suicide the summer before that accident."

"I just thought of something," Gustavo says. "Didn't you say your dad taught other paramedics? Maybe he taught the paramedics who rescued Mrs. Ridley."

"It's possible," Christopher says. "It's definitely possible."

"I wonder if Mr. Ridley and the other two passengers and the truck driver were afraid to die," Antoine says.

"We'll never know," I say. "Besides, the story said they died on impact. Maybe there wasn't time to be afraid."

"I'm afraid to die," Gustavo says. "I think my papi was afraid to die too."

"Most people in our culture are afraid to die," Eugene says.

"Are you?" Gustavo asks him.

Eugene rubs his chin. "I don't think I'm afraid, but I'm not ready to go just yet. I feel like there's still too much for me to do."

"Like helping kids?" Gustavo asks him.

"Like helping kids. And other stuff."

TWENTY-FOUR

Christopher

Eugene wants us to do something he calls *the lying-down exercise*. He asks us boys to move the table we've been sitting at to the side of the room.

"That's so sexist!" Abby says. "Asking the boys to move the table! Why didn't you ask me to help?"

Antoine and I release our grip on the table. "Good point," I tell Abby. "Go ahead. It's all yours."

Gustavo shrugs and mutters something about how it's customary for Chilean men to do the tough chores.

"I bet that since your dad died your mom's been doing plenty of tough chores," Abby points out.

So that's how Abby and Gustavo end up moving the table to the side of the room.

"You okay with the boys laying out the yoga mats on the floor?" Eugene asks Abby.

"All yours," she tells us. "Besides, it's an easy job. You should be able to handle it."

"I purposely kept the lying-down exercise for the second day," Eugene explains. "It's a way to let your bodies integrate some of what your minds have been absorbing this weekend. But I should warn you—you may not enjoy it very much."

"Too bad Jessie isn't here," Abby says. "*Lying* is her specialty."

Gustavo is putting out the last yoga mat. "I keep thinking about Jessie. She did say she was sorry. And she signed Christopher's document."

Abby stretches her arms out behind her. I know better than to ask if moving the table was a strain. "Are you saying we should forgive her?" she asks Gustavo.

"I guess what I'm saying is that we should *think* about forgiving her," he says.

The lying-down exercise sounds easy. All we have to do is lie down with our arms at our sides, our palms facing upward, and relax.

Eugene shuts off the overhead lights and pulls down the window shades. I wonder if Jessie is still sitting in the bus shelter. I also wonder if I can do what Gustavo suggested— *think* about forgiving Jessie. I don't think I can.

I can't help snickering when I notice that even though Gustavo is lying down, he has found a way to raise his hand. "Eugene, are we supposed to close our eyes or keep them open?"

"Either way works," Eugene says.

I'm starting to see that Eugene doesn't divide the world up into what's right and what's wrong the way most adults I know do. It could be the thing I like most about him.

Gustavo turns his head toward me. "What's so funny?"

"Look at your arm."

"That is kind of funny." Gustavo lowers his arm.

"It must be what the guys in Chile do," Abby says from her mat. She chuckles at her own joke.

I half expect Eugene to tell us to settle down, but he doesn't. The classroom gets quiet anyway. Are the others also suddenly more aware of the sounds around us—the cars zipping by on Sherbrooke Street, and one of the window shades flapping in the breeze?

Eugene lowers himself onto a mat. I should have known he'd be doing the exercise too.

"This feels kinda weird," Abby says. "What are we supposed to be doing exactly?"

I'm wondering the same thing.

"Nothing. That's the whole point," Eugene tells her. "To get in touch with how we're feeling."

Yesterday I think I would have said I wasn't interested in getting in touch with how I was feeling. But I feel a little different today. Abby is right. This is kinda weird. But going for the silent walk and making the mask felt weird too, and those exercises turned out to be, well…not a total waste.

In the background I hear Eugene wheezing. Does he have hay fever? If he did, wouldn't I have noticed by now?

"Spread out your fingers," Eugene tells us. "This exercise is all about relaxation. Grievers need to give themselves permission to relax—and surrender."

I like the word *surrender*. When I was a kid, my friends and I used to play army in the field across the street from my house. Our parents never liked the game. They thought it wasn't politically correct. We used water pistols and plastic swords for weapons. The goal was to get the other side to surrender.

Sometimes when a chess player loses a game, he takes his king off the board and lays him on his side. That's also called surrendering.

"Pay attention to your breathing." Eugene's voice sounds like it's coming from underwater. The wheeze is still there.

I breathe in more deeply than usual. I think about my bed at home and last night's dream. I think about all the *could haves, should haves, would haves* and *what ifs* that usually fight for space in my mind. I hope Eugene is right and that one day I'll stop wondering about those things altogether.

Isn't this exercise supposed to make us relax? But it's as if I have an itch I need to scratch. What if I only scratch a little—the way you do with an itchy scab? If you scratch too hard, you end up bleeding and the healing has to start all over.

"Be gentle with yourselves," Eugene whispers.

I don't scratch at the scab with my fingernails. I just rub around it to relieve the itchiness. I *should have* known Dad was suffering from PTSD. I *could have* gotten him help. If I'd gone down to the basement sooner, things *would have* been different. *What if* I hadn't listened to Mom and I'd gone downstairs to check on him the night he did what he did— the night he committed suicide?

I take another deep breath in, then a deep breath out. None of that matters. My dad is dead. There's nothing I can do to change that.

I picture two paramedics using the Jaws of Life to get Dolores Ridley out of the wreckage. Maybe Gustavo was right, and my dad helped train those paramedics.

Yes, my dad committed suicide because he had untreated PTSD. And yes, I will have to live with knowing that for as long as I live.

But there's something I had forgotten. Something the newspaper story helped me remember.

Paramedics are heroes.

My dad was a hero.

TWENTY-FIVE

Abby

Surrender?

He's gotta be kidding.

I was actually starting to relax—until Eugene mentioned that word.

Everyone knows surrendering means giving up. If there's one thing my mom taught me, it's never to surrender. Right up until she took her last breath, my mom fought to stay alive.

I'd like to jump up from my mat and say so, but I don't want to spoil the exercise for the boys, who seem to be getting into it. In fact, I think Antoine's asleep.

When I turn my head to one side, I see Christopher, his palms facing up, his eyelids fluttering. Gustavo is on my other side. At first I think he could be sleeping too, but when I turn to look at him, he lifts one hand off the ground and waves at me. I wave back.

Eugene wants us to pay attention to our breathing. I pay attention to Eugene's breathing instead. He doesn't sound so good.

"Just relax," Eugene tells us. I can't because now I'm thinking about my mom's last day. How it got harder for her to breathe. And how hard she tried not to surrender.

Mom didn't want to be hospitalized. *Not until they have a new heart for me*, she always said.

I pleaded with Dad to let her stay home like she wanted. But he was the one who insisted we bring her to the hospital. She was having trouble managing the stairs—and we couldn't move her downstairs because there's no bathroom there. "I can help her on the stairs," I told him. "I'll walk behind her."

Dad shook his head and said, "It's getting to be too much for us, Abby."

That was when I lost it. "It's not getting to be too much for us. It's getting to be too much for you," I said.

Mom wasn't speaking much by then—it took too much energy for her to talk—but when I started shouting, I could see her eyes darting from my face to Dad's. I knew she wanted me to apologize for shouting. But I was too angry to apologize.

That's how Mom ended up spending the last ten days of her life in Pavilion B at the Jewish General Hospital. Now, whenever we drive along Côte-des-Neiges Street, I turn away when we pass the hospital. I'm afraid that if I look, my eyes will land on the window of the sixth-floor room she died in.

The thing I hated most about that room wasn't the narrow hospital bed or even the smell of the bedpan full of pee or worse. It was a framed photo on the wall. A photograph of a rainbow over some stupid snowcapped mountain. What I hated so much about that photo was knowing someone had hung it there to cheer people up—not only patients, but also visitors like me. To give us hope that when someone we love dies, they'll cross over a rainbow and be greeted by some old guy with a long white beard, wearing a white nightshirt. When we all know that is so never going to happen. You know how I know for sure? Because if there *was* a God, he'd never have let my mom catch that virus from me, the one that weakened her heart, and he'd have made sure her name came up on time on the transplant list.

Once, a nurse looking after my mom had caught me eyeballing that photo. *You know what they say, dear?* she said. *There's a rainbow in every cloud.*

Shove your rainbow, I told her.

The nurse had gasped. I didn't apologize to her either.

After Mom was hospitalized, Dad made me keep going to school, even if there wasn't much point in my being there. I couldn't concentrate on anything the teachers said and I didn't take a single note.

All I did all day was think about my mom and wait for the afternoon bell to ring. Then I'd hop on my bike and head straight to the hospital. When I'd walk into the room, Dad would be sitting on the armchair next to her bed, reading the newspaper.

Once I caught him scanning the obituaries. *Why are you reading that crap?* I asked him. I was angry because I figured he was planning the wording for Mom's death notice.

That was the only time I ever saw my dad cry. He didn't cry when we found out how the virus had affected Mom's heart. He didn't even cry at her funeral. But at the hospital, he'd looked up from the obituary page and tears were streaming down his cheeks. *I'm checking to see if someone died, someone not too old, someone who might have signed their donor card.* He could hardly get the words out.

"Be gentle with yourselves," Eugene is saying.

If I were a different sort of person, I'd have comforted Dad when he was crying, or at least passed him the Kleenex box from Mom's tray. Or apologized for being mean. But that's not my style.

I'm not gentle.

Especially not with my dad.

But that isn't what Eugene is talking about. He's telling us to be gentle with *ourselves*. How does that even work?

I should be grateful my mom died on a Sunday. Otherwise I'd have been at school, waiting for the bell. Her skin was so thin and pale it looked like tissue paper, and she didn't have the strength to keep her eyes open.

My dad was standing at one side of the bed. I was on the other. We were each holding one of her hands. I remember that her hand felt cool and dry. "It's okay, Dorothy," my dad told her. "You can go if you have to."

My mom couldn't make words, but she turned her head slowly from side to side on her pillow. She was telling Dad she didn't have to go—that she could hold on until there was a donor heart. She wasn't ready to surrender.

"Don't go," I told her. Then I said something I had never said to either of my parents before. I didn't say I loved her. I told my mom I needed her, that I would always need her.

She tried to say something—I know because her lips were moving—but she couldn't get the words out. Then her hand went limp, and I knew she was dead.

My dad shouldn't have told her she could go. He shouldn't have let her surrender.

I don't know how to be gentle. I only know how to be tough.

I concentrate on my breathing.

My mom was tough and gentle at the same time.

I don't think I'll ever find a way to be like that.

And now that I have started to cry, it feels like I will never stop.

TWENTY-SIX

Christopher

I don't know what to do when Abby starts to bawl.

If this were chess, I'd be able to see the possibilities and work out my best move.

But being in the same room as a crying girl is considerably harder than playing chess.

I hope Eugene will realize it's time to end the lying-down exercise. For a second I wish Jessie was still here. She would do whatever it is girls do when another girl starts crying. Like give Abby a hug or say something cheesy.

But Jessie isn't here. So I start thinking about how ticked off Abby got when Eugene assumed moving a table was a job for boys. If a girl can move furniture, shouldn't a boy be able to comfort a girl who's crying? Even a boy who doesn't have much experience in that department?

"Where in your body do your feel your grief?" Eugene is asking us.

Abby sobs harder.

"It's good to cry," Eugene says quietly. "Crying lets the sadness out."

I always thought crying was a sign of weakness, and that boys who cry are wusses. Maybe Eugene is letting Abby cry because he thinks it will help let her sadness out.

When Abby curls up, clutching her elbows and still sobbing, I decide I have to do something. I roll onto my side and move my mat until I am only a few inches from her. She's rubbing her shoulders. Could that be where her body feels the grief?

"Abby." Since I don't know what else to say, I just keep saying her name.

Abby still sobs, but less noisily, and I wonder if having me there could be helping. I feel my throat get tight. To be completely honest, I'm worried I might start crying too. No one ever warns you that crying can be contagious.

I try to do what Eugene has asked—to locate where in my body I feel grief. My brain says this is a useless exercise. How can a body grieve? But I scan my body anyhow. I wriggle my toes. They feel fine. No grief there. My calves are sore, but that's from not stretching before a run. In my head, I move up my legs and into my abdomen and chest. It's when I get to my neck that I start to understand what Eugene means. My neck feels hot and sore, like it did when I was six and I had tonsillitis.

I bring my hands to my throat. It suddenly hurts too much to swallow.

Be gentle with yourselves. Eugene said that before too, but he never explained what it meant.

I don't rub my throat the way Abby rubbed her shoulders before. I just let my hands rest on either side. I think more about what Eugene said about letting the sadness out. My palms feel heavy. Are there are other ways to let the sadness out besides crying?

"I want you to lean on one elbow and slowly move into a seated position," Eugene tells us.

He doesn't tell us to open our eyes, so I keep mine closed. I hear Eugene wheeze as he adjusts himself on his mat. I hear him say, "Crap!" At first, I think I've heard wrong. *Crap* isn't exactly a swearword, and I've noticed that Eugene doesn't have the best vocabulary, but somehow I don't expect him to say *Crap*—not at a grief retreat anyhow.

I open my eyes. Eugene is wincing and shaking out his arm. Part of me must still be thinking about the lying-down exercise because I wonder whether Eugene is feeling his own grief in his arm. His mother died many years ago, but is it possible that Eugene's body still feels the loss?

Another part of me is wondering if something's wrong with Eugene. As in seriously wrong.

I don't bother leaning on my elbow the way Eugene told us to. Instead I spring up from my mat. Eugene's face is drenched in sweat, and he's taking short breaths.

"Eugene!" I can hear the fear in my own voice. "Are you okay?"

Eugene is still wincing. "My arm," he says, "and my stomach. It must've been something I had for breakf—"

Eugene is trying to prop himself up when he keels over. His body drops heavily to the floor. His chin is wet with drool. And he must have bitten his tongue when he fell, because blood is trickling from the side of his mouth.

"*Dios mio,*" Gustavo says. "What do we do?"

"Is he having a heart attack?" Antoine asks.

Eugene's skin is the same pasty white as my dad's was when I found him in the basement. For a second, that picture—walking into the basement and finding my dad dead—flashes through my mind. I blink to make the picture go away. I can't let myself think about that now. I need to focus on Eugene.

A surge of energy courses through my body. And suddenly everything around me looks more clear, almost magnified, or as if someone has turned on the lights. Eugene's eyes are closed. His cheeks are drenched in sweat.

The other kids are gathering around us. Antoine puts his hand on Eugene's chest. "He's not breathing," he says.

"Does that mean he's dead?" Gustavo asks.

Abby leans over Eugene. "Don't die!" she tells him. "You can't die."

"Someone call 9-1-1 *now,*" I hear myself say. "Tell them Eugene has had a heart attack." This time, I don't hear any fear in my voice. Instead, I sound like someone who knows what he's doing. I may not be old enough to be a paramedic, but I lived with a paramedic long enough to know what he would do if he were here.

"I'm on it," Antoine says. I hear him tapping the numbers on his cell, then speaking to the dispatcher. "A man has had a heart attack. We're on the second floor at Lawrence Academy on Sherbrooke Street…"

Every second counts.

I remember seeing a defibrillator when I came into the school yesterday morning. "Gustavo, get the defibrillator from downstairs."

"What's a defibrillator?" Gustavo asks.

"It's in a white box by the office. It says *defibrillator* on it in red letters. Go! Now!" I tell him.

I slap Eugene's face. Harder than I need to, but he's not coming to.

I pull his shirt over his head. The hair on his chest is curly and white. I start doing chest compressions. I put one hand on top of the other and begin applying pressure. I need to do this thirty times. "One, two, three…" I count out loud.

Abby is next to me, counting with me. "Eight, nine, ten…"

Now that Abby is counting, I can pray—even though I have never prayed before. *Don't let Eugene die. Please, God, if you're up there somewhere, save Eugene.*

"Eugene! Wake up!" I shout, even though I know shouting won't help. Eugene can't hear me.

What's taking the paramedics so long? And where's Gustavo with the defibrillator?

I don't tell the others what I know. Medically, Eugene is dead. And if he doesn't come to in the next five minutes, there'll be no second chance.

TWENTY-SEVEN

Abby

If it wasn't for Christopher, I'd freak out.

He's so calm it's spooky. And his calmness helps keep the rest of us calm too. Who knew calm could be catchy?

Eugene has had a heart attack. He toppled over like a Jenga tower when he was getting up from his yoga mat. And now he isn't breathing. I don't dare ask what we're all wondering: could Eugene be dead?

But if he's dead, why would Christopher be doing chest compressions?

Thank God Christopher knew where the school's defibrillator was. Gustavo's gone to get it.

It's so weird that five minutes ago, I was lying on my mat, crying. Eugene wanted us to find the place in our body where we feel our grief. Mine was in my shoulders. But now the exercise seems so unimportant. All that matters is Eugene. What if he dies? What if he's already dead?

Every single thing can change in a millisecond. Like the
moment we learned Mom's heart was so weak she would
not be able to survive without a transplant, or the moment
she passed from being alive to being dead.

Antoine is still on the phone with 9-1-1. The operator is giving him instructions, which he is calling out to
Christopher. Only from what I can tell, Christopher is way
ahead of the operator. "He's already begun applying pressure to Eugene's chest," I hear Gustavo say. "Yes, the school
has a defibrillator, and one of our friends has already gone
to get it. The school's on Sherbrooke Street in Westmount.
Didn't I say that already?"

I run out to the stairway to see if Gustavo is on his way
up. "I don't see him," I shout from the corridor.

When I get back inside the classroom, Christopher
is still doing chest compressions. "Twenty-seven, twenty-
eight, twenty-nine, thirty…" I have no idea if I am helping
Christopher by counting every time he applies pressure to
Eugene's chest. I don't know what else to do, just that I have
to do something.

When I get to thirty, Christopher stops the chest compressions and lets his arms drop to his sides. "Where's the defibrillator?" he asks, and I realize he was so focused on Eugene
that he didn't hear me when I was out in the corridor.

"Gustavo should be here with it any second."

"Okay." Now Christopher pinches Eugene's nostrils and
pulls his mouth open. Then he leans his face over Eugene's
and starts doing mouth-to-mouth resuscitation. It isn't nice

of me to think this—not when Eugene could be about to die, could even already be dead—but I wouldn't want to give mouth-to-mouth resuscitation to someone who was wearing so much bad aftershave.

Christopher's face is sweating now too.

The mouth-to-mouth resuscitation is not working.

I turn to Antoine. "Ask them where the paramedics are!"

At least I can hear Gustavo racing up the stairs. Finally! He rushes in through the classroom door. My dad, Raquel, Christopher's mom and Antoine's maman are behind him.

"*Dios mio*," Raquel says. She squats down on the floor near Eugene and starts praying in Spanish and making the sign of the cross over her chest.

"Move!" Christopher barks at her. "The defibrillator!"

Raquel gets out of the way, but now she wants to hug Gustavo. She must not be thinking straight. Doesn't she see he's got the defibrillator?

I grab the white plastic box from Gustavo. I expect it to be bigger, but it's about the size of a laptop. I open the box. A paper with a diagram on it falls out. "I don't need that," Christopher says when he sees the paper. "Give me the razor."

I don't ask what the razor is for. Christopher takes it from me and begins shaving two spots on Eugene's chest— on his left side, over and around his heart, and on the right, just above his nipple. Tufts of curly white hair fall onto the yoga mat. "If I don't shave him, the defibrillator will fry the hair instead of shocking his heart," Christopher explains.

When I notice that Christopher's hands are shaking, my own heart starts pumping harder in my chest. Maybe Christopher isn't as calm as I thought.

Now I hear a strange robotic voice saying, "Apply the adhesive electrode pads. Press on skin."

At first I think the paramedics have arrived. But the voice is coming from the box. "It's an automated external defibrillator," Christopher says. "It's going to walk us through the process."

We follow the robotic voice's instructions. I help Christopher with the adhesive pads. Christopher puts one on Eugene's left side. "The other one goes on the right," he tells me, "where I shaved him. Just like that. Good."

The machine's built-in heart monitor is already analyzing Eugene's heart rhythm. If it's abnormal—and we know it will be—it will prompt us to use the shock button. "The shocks send energy through the heart," Christopher says without taking his eyes off Eugene. "It basically gives the heart a slap in the face."

The robotic voice is giving us more instructions. "Shock required. Stop all compressions while shocking. Proceed with shock by pressing the Shock button."

Christopher presses down on the red Shock button.

Nothing.

"If the patient does not respond, press the Shock button again," the voice tells us.

Christopher presses down on the Shock button a second time.

Still nothing.

I hear Raquel praying in the background. Someone—I'm not sure who—has begun to cry. Antoine is leaning out the window. Some kids from another classroom down the hall have come to see if they can do anything to help. "The paramedics are here. I see the ambulance!" Antoine calls out. "They're pulling up outside."

"If the patient is still not responding, press the Shock button again," the voice says.

Christopher shakes his head. "I don't know why it isn't working." He sounds discouraged.

"Hit the button!" Antoine shouts.

I know we can't afford to lose even a second, so I lean in and press down on the Shock button.

We are all watching Eugene's face. It is even paler than my mom's was on the day she died.

Still nothing.

I hit the Shock button again.

I hear a moan. At first I'm confused, and I think maybe it was me. But no, it's Eugene. Thank God. He isn't dead.

Christopher sighs, and at the same second, Eugene opens his eyes. When I see his chest move ever so slightly up and down, I know he is breathing on his own again.

Everything can change in a millisecond.

When did the paramedics arrive? How could I not have noticed them coming into the classroom? But they are in the classroom now too. A man and a woman.

Christopher and I move out of the way so the female paramedic can examine Eugene. Her partner is rolling a stretcher over.

After the woman has loosened the pads from Eugene's chest, she looks from Christopher to me. "Good job, kids," she says. "It looks to me like you saved this gentleman's life."

The paramedics load Eugene onto the stretcher and tell us they're taking him to the Montreal Heart Institute. "He'll probably need an angioplasty," the male paramedic explains as he and his partner roll the stretcher out of the classroom. "But he's gonna make it."

My dad's engineering skills come in handy, because he is able to help the paramedics maneuver the stretcher down the narrow stairway. He warns them about a sharp corner and tells them exactly how many more steps they will need to take before they reach the landing.

Raquel goes to get Eugene's home phone number from the office. She'll telephone his wife so she can meet him at the Heart Institute. The rest of us follow the stretcher outside to the ambulance.

From the corner of my eye I spot Jessie. She has crossed back to our side of the street and is watching from the curb. She shouldn't be here. She knows we kicked her out. "What do you think—" I start to shout, but then I stop myself. I can't fight with her now.

Camila must have heard the commotion, because she comes running outside just as the paramedics are loading the stretcher onto the ambulance.

She rushes over to Eugene and pokes his cheek. "Are you dead?" she asks Eugene. She bites down on her lower lip. "Don't be dead."

Eugene hasn't said a word since his heart gave out. But now he manages to lift his hand from his side—and give Camila a thumbs-up.

TWENTY-EIGHT

Christopher

I hop onto the bus with Eugene. "Someone's phoning his wife now," I tell the paramedics as they lock the stretcher into position. "She'll meet him at the hospital. I could ride in the back if you think it might be helpful."

"It's good of you to offer," the woman paramedic says, "but we're okay. You go back to whatever it is you were doing in there."

I nearly explain that it's a grief retreat, but of course there isn't time. I hop down from the back of the bus and slam the door shut. The male paramedic is starting the vehicle. I follow the woman to the passenger side. "You remind me of someone," she says as she's closing the door behind her.

"My dad was a paramedic," I tell her. "His name was Chris W—"

"Chris Wolf," she says, finishing my sentence. "You have his eyes."

"I guess that means you knew him."

"I didn't just know him."

I suck in my breath. What is she going to say? Please, don't let it be anything about the way he died.

"I respected him. We all did."

I nod as I think about what she's just told me. "Me too."

But the woman paramedic doesn't hear me, because the siren is on and the bus has taken off down Sherbrooke Street.

That surge of energy I felt before is gone. I'm suddenly so tired I could keel over right here on the sidewalk in front of the school. I crouch down to catch my breath. Wow, I think, we nearly lost him.

Abby comes to get me. She doesn't say a word, just reaches for my hand and pulls me up.

"What happened? Is he going to be all right?" a voice asks.

What's Jessie doing here?

I'm about to say something to her, but Abby beats me to it. "We kicked you out," she tells Jessie. "For lying."

Jessie shifts her weight from one foot to the other. "Wh-when the ambulance pulled up to the school, I thought maybe it was one of you. Then I saw Eugene...on the stretcher. What happened?"

"He had a heart attack, but he's going to make it," I tell her.

Abby puts her hands on her hips. "You must've been disappointed nobody died. That would've made a great scene in your movie," she hisses.

Jessie winces. "I swear," she says quietly, "that's not what this is about. I was worried. For real."

Abby waves her hand in the air as if Jessie were a pesky mosquito. "Get out of here," she says.

"I can't go. I just can't."

Something about the way Jessie says it makes me look into her eyes. She meets my gaze. She has stopped shifting. I think she means it. She can't go away.

"What just happened was hard for Jessie too," I say softly. "Maybe we're being a little too harsh."

Abby looks at me as if I've suggested we set the school on fire or rob an ATM. "Too harsh? She's a traitor."

"She signed the document."

"That's right. I signed the document," Jessie says.

Abby laughs. "Who cares about some stupid document?"

"Kids!" Raquel is calling to us from the front door of the school. I figure we're going to get sent home from grief retreat. Abby and I head back to the school. When Jessie follows us up the path, Abby turns and scowls at her.

The others are gathered in the lobby. Raquel isn't canceling the rest of grief retreat. She wants us to stay until lunchtime. Camila is clutching her mami's knee. "We're going to finish the morning together," Raquel says. "Because that's what Eugene would want. Then, when he's strong enough, we'll find a way to meet up for another half day."

Abby lifts her chin toward Jessie. "What about her?" she asks Raquel. "We voted to kick her out."

Jessie slings her backpack over her shoulder again. "She's right," she says. "I'm not supposed to be here."

"So don't just stand there. Leave!" Abby says to Jessie.

Gustavo clears his throat. "The way I see it," he says, "the morning's almost over anyhow. I don't know about the rest of you, but it feels to me like we've been through a lot together—all of us. Even if she lied, Jessie's part of our group. Kind of."

Abby shakes her head. "Lying is a big deal. This was supposed to be a safe space." She makes an arc with her hands the way Eugene did when we first talked about confidentiality. "It's not safe with her here." I can tell she's making a point of not using Jessie's name.

"I just think Eugene would want us to forgive Jessie," Gustavo says.

"He might," Antoine adds.

Abby gives me a giant eye roll when I suggest a second vote. "You can't just have another vote. That isn't how democracy works."

"I bet a lot of people wished they could have another vote after Donald Trump became president," Antoine says. "Besides, this isn't world politics—it's grief retreat. Maybe we should have a vote about having a vote."

Abby sighs. "Fine!" she says. "Let's have another vote— but not about having a vote. About whether or not we should let her stay. I think you all know how I feel."

Gustavo interrupts when Raquel starts to ask who's in favor of letting Jessie come back. "We voted with our heads down before. To avoid peer pressure," he explains.

"Well then, let's do it that way again," Raquel says. We hold the vote in the lobby. Jessie offers to wait outside. This time, she closes the door behind her. Gustavo, Antoine and Abby sit down on a bench. I move some of the flowerpots over and sit on the round table. I remember how I noticed the tulips when we came in yesterday. A lot has happened since then.

"Make sure your eyes are closed," Raquel tells us. "All right then, who's in favor of letting Jessie return to grief retreat?" Raquel asks. I raise my hand.

"Who's opposed to letting Jessie come back?"

"You can open your eyes," Raquel says. "Jessie's coming back. The vote was three against one."

We all know who the one was.

"Couldn't you at least *try* to forgive her?" Antoine asks Abby.

Abby shrugs.

Gustavo goes to tell Jessie the news. "Thank you," she says to all of us when she comes back into the lobby. For once, there is nothing forced about her smile. She taps her back pocket. "Cell phone's off. I promise."

Since it's Raquel's third year at grief retreat, she is able to take over for Eugene. She says she'll follow the notes he left upstairs. No one objects when Camila insists on joining our group too. I think we're all beginning to think of her as our hermanita.

The classroom feels empty without Eugene. But now I'm glad we didn't get sent home. It feels right to be with the other kids. Even Jessie.

"First of all," Raquel says, "Eugene is going to be okay. You did amazing—all of you—the way you worked together. But especially you two," she says to Abby and me. When Raquel starts tearing up, Camila climbs onto the table so she can pat her mami's hair. "I spoke to Eugene's wife. She asked me to thank you for her."

We're going to finish the grief-mask exercise. But before we do that, Raquel wants to give us time to talk about what happened with Eugene. "Only if you want to say something," she says. "No pressure."

"I was so scared," Gustavo says. "I don't know what I'd do if something happened to Eugene. If he died, I mean."

Raquel nods. "I know," she says. "Me too. Maybe that's the price we pay when we love someone—we can't imagine carrying on without them."

"I'm glad Christopher knew what to do," Antoine says.

I nearly tell them that I tried to get out of coming to grief retreat today. What if I hadn't been here this morning? But I catch myself—there I go, asking *what if?* again.

"Christopher kept us calm," Abby adds. I don't know why they're talking about me as if I'm not here.

"I might have seemed calm," I tell the others, "but inside, I wasn't. I swear I could feel the adrenaline rushing through my veins."

"Was it a good feeling?" Jessie asks.

"Yes…" I pause. "And no. Yes because it was exciting and it made me feel really alive. No because, well, it was really stressful. And after it was all over, I felt totally drained." I don't tell the others what I'm wondering, which is whether I'm cut out to be a paramedic. Maybe I'd be happier doing another kind of job. Maybe I could be a lawyer. I do like arguing and standing up for what's right. And I liked writing that document I made Jessie sign—even if Abby laughed about it.

The old Jessie would have jumped into the conversation by now, but this time she doesn't say anything until Raquel asks how she felt when she saw the ambulance. "Gustavo told me you were in the bus shelter," Raquel says.

"I was scared. And it was hard just being an observer—not being able to help," Jessie says.

"I thought that was your specialty. Observing…and not helping," Abby mutters.

Camila raises her hand the way her brother does. Maybe it's genetic. "I have a question. Did Eugene's heart break because he exercises too much?" she asks.

"His heart didn't break, *mi amor*. It stopped, but Christopher and Abby made it start again," Raquel says.

"Does that mean Christopher and Abby are superheroes?" Camila asks. "Superheroes save the day."

"We're not superheroes," I tell Camila.

Abby pretends to tie an invisible cape around her shoulders. "Speak for yourself, Christopher. I happen to possess superpowers—in addition to my amazing sense of humor."

Raquel wants us to put on our grief masks, then walk around the classroom and look at each other.

"Do we show our outside mask or our inside mask?" Gustavo asks.

I was wondering the same thing.

"The mask doesn't fit right if you wear it inside out," Antoine says.

"That's true," Raquel says. "If you reverse the mask, the nose will push up against your nose. It'll be slightly uncomfortable, but it's still possible. In any case, why don't we start with your outside masks?"

Phew.

"You only have to show your inside mask if you want to," Raquel adds.

Double phew. There's no way I'm showing the other kids my inside mask. Besides, isn't the whole point of having an inside mask to keep it inside? Otherwise, it would be an outside mask.

I fasten the elastic band behind my ears and look out from behind the mask. I think about how I have my dad's eyes. He tried to be strong too. But even if I have his eyes, even if I take after him in many ways, I'm not him.

"Now that your masks are on, go ahead and walk around the room. Meet each other's masks," Raquel says.

"How can a mask meet another mask?" I hear Camila ask her mom.

"It happens all the time," Raquel tells Camila. "It's called life."

The first mask I see is Gustavo's. He's cut out photos of families and mountains. There's a photo of a boy and his sister. They are not Gustavo and Camila, but they don't have to be. "Nice mask," I tell him.

"Be strong," he says, reading the words off my mask.

Antoine has made a list of video games on his outside mask. I see *2K17* and *Battlefield 1*. He's also drawn a basketball and a green box with wheels that is probably supposed to be a tank. Maybe video games are Antoine's way to escape, the way my dad disappeared into his man cave.

Abby has decorated her outside mask with *LOLs*, *LMAOs* and *HAHAHAs*. It's her way to say something about her sense of humor. Can being funny be a mask?

It's easy to understand why there's a cell phone and a camera on Jessie's outside mask. I'm not sure about the teardrop. Maybe it has to do with her parents' split.

"Now if you feel like it, and only if you feel like it," Raquel tells us, "you can switch over to your inside mask. As Antoine said, it's not going to feel that comfortable. He meant physically, but it could feel uncomfortable on an emotional level too. So like I said, only if you feel like it."

I don't feel like it.

But I am curious to see what the others have done with their inside masks. That makes me feel a little guilty. As if I am taking something from my friends without giving them something in return. I almost expect Raquel to say that if we don't want to show the others our inside masks, we can't be part of the exercise. But she doesn't.

Gustavo's inside mask has a cut-out picture of one small boy. He is alone and younger than Gustavo. I know without asking that the boy must be about the age Gustavo was when his papi died. I also understand that no matter what a good son and brother Gustavo is, no matter what kind of grown-up he becomes, part of him will always be that lonely boy.

Antoine's inside mask makes me feel even sadder. It only has one small picture in the bottom corner. An empty crib. Vincent's crib.

Abby leaves her outside mask on.

Jessie has turned hers over. But her inside mask is blank. Then I remember she wasn't here when we decorated our inside masks. Even so, her blank mask seems to be saying something. Maybe she isn't sure who she is on the inside.

I take a deep breath.

I did not expect to learn so much from seeing the others' inside masks.

I take another deep breath. Then I remove my mask and turn it around so the inside faces out.

Let the others know that I am not so strong and calm and logical as I pretend to be.

TWENTY-NINE

Abby

It feels weird to be back in the same classroom at Lawrence Academy. There's a map of the world and posters on the wall that weren't here before. And because it's November, the trees outside the window are bare. We're supposed to get our first snowstorm at the end of next week.

Eugene looks great. He is wearing the tracksuit he wore the first day of the grief retreat, only with a turtleneck instead of a T-shirt underneath. He's had his hair cut too. It's still combed over, but the combed-over pieces are shorter, so they don't look so bad.

I've seen Eugene a few times since May. Twice with Christopher when we visited him in the hospital. Then, after Eugene was back on his feet, Dad and I had a couple of private grief-counseling sessions with him.

It also feels weird to see Jessie again. I'm glad Christopher warned me she was coming. "Hi," she says when sees me.

"How you doing, Abby?" I can tell from her voice that she wants to be friends.

"I'm fine," I say. But I make a point of *not* asking how she is. I want her to know that I haven't forgiven her, that I may never forgive her.

"Sorry about taking off so abruptly back in May," Eugene jokes. "I usually make a point of saying a proper goodbye."

In the email Eugene sent around, he explained we'd only be spending the afternoon together so that we could complete the final exercise he had planned for us. He didn't say anything else about the exercise.

Christopher predicts we'll be going outside. "Why else would Eugene have told us to dress warmly?" he said to Antoine and me when we ran into him in the lobby.

Gustavo thinks it will be some sort of commemoration for our loved ones who died. "Two years ago we released blue balloons and white balloons into the sky," he says.

Antoine hopes it will be balloons. "Balloons remind me of Vincent. When Mom first brought him home from the hospital, Maman and I decorated the front door with yellow balloons. Maman didn't want us to follow the usual blue for boys, pink for girls."

Though I don't mention this to the others, I'm hoping the activity will involve art. I keep the mask I made in May on the bulletin board over my desk. I even got my dad to make a grief mask too.

The exercise does not involve going outside or making art.

Eugene wants us to write a note to our loved one who died. He hands out paper and envelopes.

"Envelopes?" I say. "Where exactly are you planning to send the letters? Postage to heaven is expensive. And postage to hell costs extra."

Jessie laughs at my crack about hell. I overheard her telling Antoine she's been seeing her dad again. That she even met his new girlfriend.

Because, as Eugene points out, not everyone is a natural-born writer, he puts a few prompts on the white-board. "No obligation to use any of them, but if you get stuck, go ahead and try them out. And if you want to add any to my list"—he waves the dry-erase marker he is using in the air—"feel free to come up to the board and jot them down for the others."

I want to tell you that...

When I think about you I feel...

These are the things I miss most about you...

These are the ways I've changed since you died...

I think you'd be glad to know that...

I need you to know that...

I never told you this...

I must be a natural-born writer, because once I start, I can't stop.

Dear Mom,

I want to tell you that I miss you every day. I miss how you used to drool when you laughed really hard, and how you didn't mind when I teased you about it.

When I think about you, I feel sad. Not just for me, but also for you, and for Dad, but mostly for you. It's November, so it's not too pretty outside, but you'd have said the air smells good, and you'd have made hot chocolate on a day like this.

I still can't look when we drive by the Jewish General Hospital. I still get upset when I think about how you didn't get a new heart in time.

But the pain is getting a little—softer. The edges don't poke at me the way they did before.

I think you'd be glad to know Dad and I are starting to get along a little better. We've even gone to see Eugene in his office a few times for counseling. And I hope it's okay with you that Dad has a friend—Gustavo and Camila's mother, Raquel (we met them at grief retreat). They're just friends, but you never know.

I never told you this: I used to think I was responsible for what happened to your heart. Remember how I had a flu just before you caught the virus? I finally told that to Eugene and Dad during one of our sessions. They said I needed to stop blaming myself. That it wasn't my fault and that some circumstances are out of our control—and that we need to accept that.

Sometimes, Mom, an hour or two go by and—I hope you won't take this the wrong way—I don't think about you.

What I'm trying to tell you, Mom, is I'm never going to stop missing you.

I'm about to sign my name when I think of one more thing I want to include in my letter.

What I've learned at grief retreat is that it's okay to never stop missing someone. That it's a sign of how much you loved them and still love them.

Always

Your Abby

I reread my letter to check for spelling and grammar mistakes (there aren't any), and then I fold it into three and put it in the envelope.

I'm not going to read my letter out loud. What I wrote is private, between me and my mom.

Maybe some kids do better at a place like grief retreat than a kid like me.

I'm not saying I hated it, only that I might be the sort of person who needs to work things out in my own way at my own pace. I don't like feeling forced into things.

Though I'd never admit it to him, I'm still glad Dad made me come here. Even if I mostly made wisecracks, I'd like the others to know I'm glad I met them.

They are still writing. So I go up to the whiteboard and add the prompt that I came up with to Eugene's list. *What I've learned at grief retreat is…*

THIRTY

Christopher

Sometimes I worry I'm getting as bad as Jessie.

I'm not saying I want to make documentaries, just that I never used to be all that interested in other people's stories.

Last week, after I beat this kid online at chess, I did something unusual for me—I wrote to ask him questions about himself. *Are you an only child? Do you have other hobbies or just chess? Do you know yet what you want to be when you grow up?*

I guess I'm becoming more curious about others. I find myself wondering, What does it feel like to be you?

For instance, right now I should be working on my letter to my dad, but I'm peeking over the other kids' shoulders, trying to see what they are writing.

Gustavo is working on some kind of journal entry. Maybe he's telling his papi how he needs to study harder for school, and how he's getting to be better friends with Abby because his mom is hanging out with Abby's dad.

Antoine probably went with the first prompt, *I want to tell you that…* I imagine he is telling Vincent all the things he wishes they'd been able to do together, like building sandcastles and playing ball hockey.

I've never seen anybody write as quickly as Abby does. She put her letter in the envelope before I could try to read it.

When Jessie notices me trying to read her letter, she raises her eyebrows as if to say *Aha, I caught you.* She must be writing to her dad, even though he isn't dead. She puts her hand over her paper so I won't be able to read it. It doesn't seem fair that a person who is so snoopy would share so little about herself.

That thought gives me the writing prompt I need.

Dear Dad,

It doesn't seem fair that I didn't have a chance to say goodbye to you.

Everything that happened—and you know I mean your suicide—doesn't feel fair.

At first I was really angry at you. I thought you were a coward for taking your own life.

But I don't think that anymore. I think you must have felt like you didn't have a choice.

I still wish there was something I could have done to stop you.

But I've met a lot of people who knew you.

I know you were a hero. Even if you committed suicide.

Everyone's always saying how much I look like you and act like you.

I look up at the whiteboard. Abby has added a prompt.

What I've learned at grief retreat is that even if we're a lot alike, even if we have the same name and the same eyes, I'm not you. And that's okay.

Your loving son,
Christopher

Eugene doesn't suggest we read our letters out loud. To be honest, I think I wouldn't have minded.

The last part of the exercise is going to take place outside. "I told you so," I say to Abby. "That's why he told us to dress warmly."

Someone has built a stone fire pit at the back of the butterfly garden. Eugene adds kindling and some logs, then throws in a match, and the fire takes.

"You can do whatever you like with the letter you just wrote. You can keep it with you always—or you can tear it into shreds. If you like, you can go ahead and throw your letter into the fire," he says.

"I want to keep my letter," Jessie says. She has folded her envelope in two and is holding it in her hands.

"That's good," Eugene tells her. "The idea behind the exercise is that what you wrote in your letters comes from here." Eugene taps his heart, and when he does I remember how grateful I was when his heart started pumping again. "When you feel something here, it's with you always."

Jessie tucks her letter into the front pocket of her black jacket. Maybe someday she'll give the letter to her dad. Jessie glances over at Abby. She's been trying to catch her eye all morning. But Abby's still ignoring her. Maybe those two weren't destined to be BFFs.

Abby, Gustavo and I toss our letters into the fire. We watch as they burst into flames, then get smaller and smaller before they turn to ash.

Antoine looks like he is still deciding what to do with his. We are all waiting for him to make up his mind. Then he turns away from the fire pit and walks toward the back fence. He squats down on the ground. It takes me a minute to realize that he is digging a small grave with his hand.

I go over to help. The two of us work together silently. It takes a while because the earth is packed hard. When the hole is deep enough, Antoine buries the letter. I pat his shoulder, and then we rejoin the others.

Eugene is carrying a cardboard box. "Things got a little confused back in May—my fault, I know. So you guys never got your mementos from grief retreat. I'm afraid they're a little worse for wear."

He rests the box on a picnic table and opens the top flaps. Inside are what's left of the tulip pots we saw when we first arrived at grief retreat. The petals are dried out and brown. No one remembered to water the plants.

"No offense," Antoine says, "but what are we supposed to do with dead plants?"

"I was hoping you'd ask." Eugene takes a pot out of the box and taps its side. "There's a bulb in here. We haven't watered the plants, so the bulbs should be nice and dry. You can plant them in your gardens or in a flowerpot on a windowsill or a deck. Best to do it soon—before the frost hits next week. By next May, there should be tulips blooming—a reminder of our time together at grief retreat."

It's time for us to meet our parents in the school lobby. I end up walking between Abby and Eugene.

"I want to thank you guys again," Eugene says, "for what you did. For giving me a second chance. Or in my case, a third chance."

"No biggie," Abby tells him.

Maybe it's because I haven't said a lot today that Eugene looks at me. "How 'bout you, Christopher Wolf? How you doin'?"

"Okay," I say. "I'm still hurting, but I'm okay."

Eugene claps my shoulder. "Okay is good."

I turn to Abby. I don't know why I didn't notice this till now, but she isn't wearing soccer cleats, just regular sneakers. "How about you?" I ask her. "You okay too?"

"Look," she says, "I don't want you guys taking this the wrong way…" Her half smile tells me we're in for one of her zingers.

"I didn't exactly love grief retreat. But yeah, I'm okay. And you know what's even better than that? Being okay with being okay."

ACKNOWLEDGMENTS

Planet Grief grew out of two feature stories I wrote for the *Montreal Gazette*: one about a Montreal grief retreat for kids, another about the emotional challenges faced by paramedics. The grief retreat I wrote about was founded by Dawn Cruchet, whom I interviewed and who has, fortunately for me, become a close friend. Special thanks to Dawn for teaching me so much about life and death and the grieving process, and also to her and her husband, Peter, for their hospitality. I didn't know when I visited the Cruchets that their son Matt was a paramedic, nor that their grandson Jacob was an avid reader. Thanks to Matt and Jacob for teaching me to use a defibrillator. Special thanks to Dawn and Jacob for reading the first draft of this book. Thanks to Danny Garvin, a long-time paramedic, who trusted me with his story. Thanks also to the Sorel family for your friendship and open hearts. I did not get to meet Todd Sorel, but I hope I captured some of his spirit in this story. Thanks to the terrific team at Orca Books, especially my extraordinarily wise and astute editor and friend Sarah Harvey. Finally, thanks to my family—my daughter, Alicia; my dad, Maximilien; my sister, Carolyn; and my brother, Michael. Together we are learning that there are many ways to grieve—and that that's a good thing.

MONIQUE POLAK is the author of more than twenty novels for kids and young adults. She has also written one nonfiction book for kids (*Passover: Festival of Freedom*), as well as a board book for toddlers. Monique is a two-time winner of the Quebec Writers' Federation Prize for Children's and Young Adult Fiction. In addition to being an active freelance journalist whose work appears regularly in the *Montreal Gazette*, Monique teaches English literature, creative writing and humanities at Marianopolis College in Montreal, Quebec. For more information, visit moniquepolak.com.